My Wonderful

The most
anyone coul

I love you so

This comes as a very
small token of my love and
much we hope it will
help you enjoy our holiday.
with all my love.
your adoring

The man trap

Detective Chief Inspector Sidney Walsh is summoned to the scene when a body is found in a bunker on the Hasling Abbey golf course.

At first, the pro-am tournament at the prestigious Hasling Abbey golf course near Cambridge appears to be going well for Robin Sainsbury and his partner, Amanda Knightly. Then disaster strikes. It is bad enough for any golfer's ball to end up in a steep-sided bunker, but to then find it clasped in the white and rigid hand of a murdered man is the stuff real nightmares are made of.

Detective Chief Inspector Sidney Walsh and his Cambridgeshire Constabulary CID team are sent to investigate. Nothing, however, proves straightforward. What on earth had Hitler, a long dead hermit Catholic priest and two National Front thugs got to do with it? What was the murdered man's beautiful model wife up to on the night he died? Was the story of a haunting ghost and an ancient family feud relevant?

Love, lust and human weakness are certainly present in abundance, with wronged husbands and fathers and even jealousy between the dead man's various mistresses, but it is not until the discovery of secret places in the dead man's Tudor home that anything starts to make sense. Even so, Sidney Walsh and his team have to go through a traumatic baptism of fire, violence and fear before the case can finally be resolved.

Books by Richard Hunt

Murder in ruins (1991)
Death sounds grand (1991)
Death of a merry widow (1992)
Deadlocked (1994)
Murder benign (1995)
A cure for killers (1995)

THE MAN TRAP

Richard Hunt

Constable · London

First published in Great Britain 1997
by Constable & Company Ltd
3 The Lanchesters, 162 Fulham Palace Road
London W6 9ER
Copyright © 1997 by Richard Hunt
The right of Richard Hunt to be
identified as the author of this work has been
asserted by him in accordance with the
Copyright, Designs and Patents Act 1988
ISBN 0 09 476840 4
Set in Palatino 10pt by
Pure Tech Corporation, Pondicherry, India
Printed and bound in Great Britain by
Hartnolls Ltd, Bodmin, Cornwall

A CIP catalogue record for this book
is available from the British Library

1

The monks of the Abbey of Hasling would never have recognised the place where they had spent their tonsured lives in organised toil and dedicated prayer. Their mellowed grey limestone buildings of elegant pillars, of soaring arched roofs and meticulous carvings, had long since disappeared.

It had all been the fault of Henry VIII, that monarch of many wives, whose marriage problems resulted in the rejection of the Roman Pope in favour of a Lutheranic sort of Protestantism, only with himself as leader and top dog. To cock a royal snook and wave two fingers at one of the most powerful men in the Western world at the time had been a brave thing to do, but needs must when the devil drives, and it did solve some of Henry's other pressing problems – it gave him the chance to get his hands on the monastic cash box.

However, brave or not, it was the major cause of a few centuries of intermittent war between several intolerant nations, and resulted in bloody conflict between reformation and counter-reformation, heretics and idolaters, engendering the religious fear and hate which still linger in many minds and places, even in our so-called enlightened modern times.

Anyway, that was why Hasling Abbey was dissolved in a spiritual sense.

In physical terms it was taken apart to become a useful source of material: much of the dressed stone was used to build or make alterations to some of nearby Cambridge's colleges, Trinity in particular, which Henry formed by uniting the even then ancient colleges of King's Hall and Michaelhouse, only a year or so before he died.

The extensive lands of the monastic demesne, however, passed into rich private hands, to become farms, parks and gardens.

Where the cloistered buildings had once stood there rose an elegant, cosy residential structure of flat red bricks with timber frames, leaded windows and soaring twisted chimneys. That first building no doubt served generations of its owners quite adequately, but then, as styles and fashions changed, it was added to, or altered, with stone and marble, until it gradually developed into the type of rambling property considered nowadays to be a beautiful historic English country house.

As time went by the land round about changed in appearance too. Enclosures meant different crops, larger fields and larger farms, and the woodlands opened up as extensive stands of oak were felled for Nelson's ships. They were dramatic enough events in their day, no doubt, but nowhere near as dramatic as when the burdens of modern death duties forced the house to become a hotel, for then the nearby farms, the lawns and gardens were all bulldozed and sculpted into a twentieth-century landscape delight – an eighteen-hole championship golf course.

It was a glorious late May morning.

The sun shone down warm and bright from a near cloudless blue sky, on to the gently undulating Hasling Abbey golf course. The deciduous trees that mingled with tall pines to line the fairways and edge the well-mown greens were all now in full summer leaf, and liberally interspersed between them were the flowering rhododendrons, a gorgeous mass of purple and red. In scrubbier places, tamed wild yellow-white lupins vied with golden gorse to add a range of different colours, and to spread a deliciously subtle sweet scent out into the faint easterly breeze.

There was a crowd of people near the first tee, many more than usual on a normal working weekday, and that was because a tournament was about to be played.

It was not, however, a tournament for local club members. This was a private one, staged by a local manufacturing company with a large international market as their main annual sales promotional event. The executives and buyers of existing and potential customers from many countries had been lured here to be wined and dined, fawned upon, flattered and lavishly entertained; in between times, those who so wished could play golf for desirable prizes.

6

Not surprisingly, the event was very well attended, for it was rated as the most important in that particular industry's social calendar. Anyone who aspired to be anyone would be there; just to be invited signified membership of an élite. For the company running it, the event was an unmitigated success. To it were due their full order books and consistent years of steadily increasing turnover, market share, profit, and other desirable statistics. They needed to do little else to promote their products.

The tournament was a pro-amateur event, played over two days. Each participating guest was partnered by a professional player. All the pairs played on the first day, but only the twelve with the lowest aggregate joint scores would play on the second day, for the prizes. Those were well worth winning. Five thousand pounds for the professional, and for the winning amateur, a full Wedgwood bone china dinner service, together with a set of Waterford cut crystal glasses.

Only a few of the professionals were well-known players, of course. Mostly they were good solid club pros, hired on a fixed fee, but the dangling carrot of the prize made them ready and willing to coach, encourage and exhort their amateur partners to achieve higher levels of performance than they would ever have thought possible. That created the element of competition which enthused those who were merely spectators, as well as those actually playing. The normal handicap system ensured that each pairing had as much chance of winning on the day as any of the others.

So, when the sun and breeze had dried the early morning dew from the first few greens, they started teeing off. That was at about eight thirty.

Robin Sainsbury was the resident professional of a Bedfordshire club. He was a sturdily built, middle-aged man of medium height, with reddish hair, keen blue eyes and a pleasant but rather sad face, and he had drawn a woman as his partner.

She was about thirty years old, five foot eight or so in height, with short dark hair. She was wearing stylish fawn slacks and a white woollen jumper, both of which clearly displayed a neat, trim figure. Her eyes were dark and intelligent but cold, in a pretty enough face that was frowningly serious and determined. It also looked a little tired and nervous.

She was, Robin Sainsbury decided, after a quick all-embracing glance which did not fail to take in the mobile telephone clipped to her golf bag, probably a career woman, one who worked hard to achieve success in whatever she did. She wore no wedding ring. He feared that she might be one of those women whose battle cry was *Equality*, in a one-sided war against the males of mankind; but it was unwise and unfair to make snap judgements about people. If she possessed a desire to succeed and to win, that would be useful in his own quest, which was to take the professional's prize for himself.

'Miss Amanda Knightly – Robin Sainsbury.' The official at the first tee made the introductions. 'Miss Knightly is a sixteen handicap at her club in Bristol. Robin is a scratch player, of course. You tee-off seventh, that'll be at about twenty past nine. Now, local club rules apply. With mixed pairs the men play off first, from the back tee, then you can all move up to the ladies' tee. That saves a lot of time. The best of luck, then. Oh yes, and do please try and steer clear of the gardens down the left, on the seventh. They're out of bounds of course, but we're having a bit of trouble with some of the occupiers.'

Robin Sainsbury proffered his hand in greeting and at the same time gave Miss Amanda Knightly one of the friendly smiles he gave to all those who came to him for professional tuition. For one awful moment he thought that both were going to be ignored, for she looked bewildered and confused at the sight of the outstretched hand; eventually, however, a half-smile seemed to flicker round her lips, and then a cool soft hand reached out to briefly touch his own.

'Have you played in a tournament like this before?' Sainsbury asked as they moved over to join the queue of waiting players.

'No,' she admitted with a slight shake of her head, and in a voice that was surprisingly light and girlish.

Sainsbury nodded thoughtfully. That would explain her strained and stiff attitude. She was bound to be nervous at the prospect of driving off with so many people watching her, but nerves tensed the muscles and played havoc with a golf swing. He looked down at his wrist-watch: he had about fifteen minutes to try and boost her self-confidence.

'Is there any part of your game that you're not happy with?'

Amanda Knightly's face twitched a bit, as though reluctant to admit having any weaknesses at all. 'I'm not too good with the driver,' she admitted eventually.

8

'You, and a few million others,' Robin responded cheerfully while having a look at the set of clubs in her bag. They were fairly new and not all that expensive, but at least they were a matched set. 'Do a couple of practice swings. Maybe I can help?'

Amanda dutifully obliged. She pulled the driver out of her bag, set her feet apart, addressed an imaginary ball, waggled the club-head a few times, then executed her swing.

Robin pursed his lips. She was trying to hit far too hard, but her grip and her stance were just about all right. If this were to be only a practice session then he might have suggested some minor adjustments to them, but under the circumstances it would be better to deal only with one problem at a time.

'That's not bad,' he said encouragingly, 'but you're snatching a little when you start your down-swing; that gets your hands coming down in front of the club-head. Have another go. Take the club-head back nice and steady, then count one, two at the top of the swing. Keep your head really still. Timing is much more important than brute power.'

Amanda Knightly had another go.

'Well done! That's much better. You're more in control of the club-face now, aren't you? Try it with an iron. Not too hard, let the club-head do the work. That's very good.'

If she didn't try and thump the ball out of sight every time, she might be more accurate with her direction. There was little else he could do in such a short time. Unfortunately the girl didn't really seem to be concentrating all that hard on what she was doing, and achieving that five thousand pounds prize money was beginning to seem a bit like a pipe dream.

'Number seven pair to the tee, please,' someone called out in an already hoarse voice.

Now it was their turn for a public introduction and the tense business of getting a competition round started.

The first hole was a short par three, with the pin set well left of centre on a raised kidney-shaped green, where it was guarded on either side by steep-faced sand traps.

Robin Sainsbury played solidly and safely into the middle of the green. His ball came to rest about twenty feet from the hole. He would have a chance of a birdie, but at worst he ought to get down in two for his par; and that would be a fair start to his

9

round. Their two male opponents drove off, then the group made its way forward to the ladies' tee.

'Take a nice easy swing with your five iron. Aim for the middle of the green,' Robin advised.

Amanda's cheeks were pink with the embarrassment of being the centre of attention, but she nodded nervously and made a couple of practice swings, either of which would have been ideal. She then addressed the ball, gritted her teeth, and proceeded to do what Robin was afraid she might – she tried to hit the ball out of sight. The result was a gigantic slice. The ball screamed its curving way out towards the trees on the right, then started to swing back in. It was still travelling fast when it hit the ground six feet from the left-hand bunker. From there it bounced up into the clinging thick grass at the top edge of the sand trap and lost most of its momentum. It might easily have rolled back into the sand, but it didn't; instead it trickled gently down the far slope, and ended up four feet from the hole.

'Great! Good shot,' Sainsbury exclaimed dutifully. If luck like that persisted, they could win any tournament, but it wouldn't – golf wasn't that kind of game. Still, you made your own luck in life sometimes, if you had enough determination. So he took great pains to study the contours of the green, and to line up his own putt as methodically and precisely as he could. Judging the pace was going to be more difficult on this first green than getting the line right. It would be too easy to run three or four feet past, or leave it tantalisingly short.

He swung the putter gently, then experienced that indescribable feeling of elation that golf is all about. His ball teetered on the left edge of the hole, hesitated, then dropped in.

When it was her turn, he helped Amanda line up her putt, talking calmly and quietly all the time. She seemed more composed with a putter in her hand, and only seemed marginally surprised when her ball rattled into the hole.

The second was a dog-legged par four, possibly the most difficult hole on the course, except perhaps for the seventh, the twelfth and the sixteenth. Robin gave his drive a touch of draw to bring his ball round the bend and into the light rough on the far side of the fairway. His second, with a three iron, took a favourable bounce on a down slope, and the ball rolled on and on, through the gap between the bunkers, to the front apron of the green.

Amanda's thumping drive this time was a low curving hook into the tall trees at the dog-leg bend. In there it ricocheted from one trunk, bounced on a sturdy branch or two, and ended up going straight through the wood to an ideal position on the other side. She topped her three wood second shot, but hit it sufficiently hard for it to bumble along far enough to leave her only a simple eight iron chip to the green. That was hit far too hard, but fortunately she got well under it, sending the ball soaring upwards to the heavens, whence it returned almost vertically to thud into the turf of the green a mere three feet from the pin.

On another occasion Robin might have laughed light-heartedly, and made some joke about beginners, or the devil looking after his own, but that would not be wise in this case – besides, he needed all his concentration to putt his own ball up to beside the hole and make an easy par. The excitement, however, seemed to be overcoming his partner's coldness or mental preoccupation. Success with the golf club does have the effect of making a player's world seem warm and rosy. When Amanda's ball dropped in the hole, she waved her arms in the air in delight, and her face became so animated that it was now radiantly pretty. She was becoming more attractive by the minute, or so it seemed to Robin Sainsbury.

The tournament's seventh pairing may have only completed two holes, but they had commenced two rounds of golf that were to become much talked of afterwards, by the increasingly large number of spectators who, drawn by the cheers and sounds of applause, were now following them round.

Amanda's luck with the driver and her fairway irons continued, much to the delight of the enlarged gallery. She cleared bunkers by inches and bounced her ball off trees or out-of-bounds fences into ideal positions on open fairways, but her success with her putter was genuinely earned, and that made her even more bright-eyed and vivacious.

Not everything went quite right, of course. There were occasions when a shank or unlucky bounce put her into serious trouble, but then the course-wise Robin Sainsbury was able to play the rule book, by pointing at the scrapings of some animal, or finding dubious signs of ground under repair, to give her an

11

advantageous free drop away from the worst of the trouble, to enable a satisfactory recovery shot to be made.

Robin Sainsbury himself was playing very well too. He was a very creditable three under par by now, but their combined score, with her handicap adjusted, was ridiculously low. It was fortunate that they had so many spectators as witnesses, or else their score cards might well have been disbelieved.

It was on the eighteenth hole, another par four, where the fairway ran wide and straight towards a spacious green and the sprawling pile of the country house hotel, when Amanda's luck ran out. Perhaps it was the additional crowd of people on the hotel's bar veranda that put her off. Whatever it was, this time her approach shot failed to clear a deep steep-backed bunker, and her ball fell from the heavens with an ominous thud, plugging itself deep in the sand.

'This really is a tricky one,' Robin murmured.

Indeed, that was the understatement of the century. A plugged ball, so close to such a steep bank, was a golfer's nightmare. Even a sideways or backwards shot was not practical, since there was hardly any room to swing the club.

'Just concentrate on trying to get it up and out of the bunker. Don't worry where it ends up. It couldn't be in a worse place than it is. Dig your feet in and get a good firm footing, then hit the sand about an inch behind the ball. About there,' he added, pointing down with his finger. 'You can hit it as hard as you like this time.'

He did not say that there was no way, short of a miracle, that she was going to get that ball out from there. The best that could happen was that the ball would hit the bank and bounce back to an easier spot. He'd seen really good players take half a dozen strokes from situations like this, and end up by tearing their hair out with frustration.

Amanda was all serious of face now. She shuffled her feet deep into the soft sand to get a firm stance, then set about waggling the club-head nervously over the desired spot. Then she drew the club back and swung at the ball with all her might.

It might well have been a good shot, in spite of Robin Sainsbury's pessimism. However, as the club-face hit the sand it unaccountably seemed to stop dead. Amanda felt a jarring pain run up her wrists and forearms that broke her grip and allowed the club to fly out of her hands. That was an awful enough experience, but there was worse to follow. Where she'd hit the sand there was now revealed the sight of a white human hand, and in it, clasped loosely in its claw-like fingers, was her ball.

A series of convulsive, high-pitched screams burst out from Amanda's open mouth. She could not drag her gaze away from the dreadful sight, yet her desperate need to put distance between herself and what she saw sent her staggering backwards out of the bunker. While doing that her feet disturbed more sand, and revealed part of a human face – a nose, an eye and an ear. That was enough to cut her wild screeches down to gulping croaks, and after one more desperately mournful howl, that tough career woman effected a good old-fashioned Victorian swoon, collapsing senseless on the grass at Robin Sainsbury's feet.

He too stared in horror and disbelief at the grisly sight exposed in the bunker.

'Christ Almighty! We ought to get a free drop for that,' he muttered to no one in particular. Which only goes to show how single-minded and dedicated golf professionals are. Nevertheless he felt a sickening tightening in his stomach, which needed an effort to control. When the spasm had passed, he walked over to Amanda's golf bag, picked up her mobile telephone, and proceeded to press the 9 button three times. Then he went back to sit on the grass by the distraught girl, to help her sit up and to provide the sympathetic shoulder she needed to cry on.

'Are you sure the man's dead?' the police duty sergeant asked, having gone through the *Who are you?* and *Where are you?* routines, and having already passed the necessary message to divert the nearest patrol car to the Hasling Abbey Hotel and golf course.

'Well, he's not showing much sign of life, and neither would you if you'd been lying in a bunker with your head under the sand,' Robin Sainsbury replied sharply. It may have sounded flippant, but there was no humour in his voice. He might have added that he ought to know a dead person when he saw one, but that wouldn't have been strictly true. The only dead people he'd ever seen, until now, had been his great-grandad, when he'd gone with his mother to pay their last respects, and more recently his wife Janet, whose painfully pale and haggard face

13

had hardly been recognisable as that of the pretty vivacious girl he'd married ten years earlier. The cancer had eaten away the bloom of her youth and had left her . . . well, it was better not to try and remember that last sight he'd had of her. Perhaps he should find out if the body in the bunker had a pulse, but there were other people milling around oohing and ahing, who could do that if they wanted. He was content to stay on the grass where he was, with Amanda Knightly's arms flung tightly round his neck, her still flooding tears running down his chest and drenching his shirt. Janet had been the last armful of warm womanhood he'd had to console and cuddle, and that had been a long long time ago. It was strangely pleasant to be doing it again.

He'd almost forgotten that he was still holding a phone.

'I'll have to get the doctor there anyway,' he heard the duty sergeant say.

'Please yourself. I'll be here by the eighteenth green.'

He put the phone down beside him on the grass. He could use that hand to better purpose by holding the girl tighter, by running his fingers through her lightly scented hair, and wiping away the unmanly tears that were forming in his own eyes as long-subdued feelings came flooding back.

2

When the dead body of a lesser animal is found lying about, it will very soon attract the attention of flies, and scavengers of all shapes and sizes. However, if the body happens to be one of the human variety, then the most notable species to swarm round it will be the police.

The first of those will almost certainly be the occupants of the nearest police patrol or panda car, whose initial task is to confirm whether or not the 999 call is genuine.

If it is, the next to arrive should be the scene of crime team. These are the photographers, fingerprint experts and all those other forensic science specialists who are trained to find, preserve and identify all the evidence on the body and the site.

After them will come the officers of the Criminal Investigation Department, who, as their name implies, will be responsible for seeking out the perpetrators of a crime, if it should turn out that a crime has in fact been committed. They will set out to identify the corpse, find and question any witnesses, and clarify the sequence of relative events.

Death may, of course, result from natural causes, accident, suicide or murder, and it is not always a simple matter to tell which of those applies in any particular case, unless there's a knife sticking out of the body's back, or a garrotte still tight round its neck; deciding which is a matter for the Crown's coroner. That he will do when he has received the report of a Home Office pathologist, and been given all the appropriate forensic evidence gathered from the site, or elsewhere.

On that lovely May morning, the appropriate Cambridgeshire Constabulary officers lost no time in making their way to Hasling Abbey and its eighteenth green. Only the leader of the Criminal Investigation Department, Detective Chief Inspector

Sidney James Walsh, was unable to respond immediately to the confirmed 999 call. He was tied up with family matters, and was visiting his wife in Addenbrooke's Hospital, because the evening before she had undergone a hysterectomy operation. At such times duty takes second place, and so it was nearly an hour later before he felt free to set out for the Hasling Abbey Hotel.

Detective Chief Inspector Sidney James Walsh was a fit-looking man in his early fifties, about six feet tall and sturdily but not heavily built. His eyes were brown, and so once had been his hair, but that was now substantially greyed. He had a reasonably good-looking, somewhat rugged face, which generally held a serious expression, no doubt the result of having been exposed so long to the darker, more unpleasant side of human behaviour. However, there were some wrinkles and creases round his eyes and mouth which suggested that the ability to laugh had not been entirely suppressed.

Most of the spaces in the hotel car-park were occupied when he arrived, but that presented him with no problems. A young uniformed constable was there who presumably recognised him, since he waved and pointed out a vacant spot.

'They're all down there, sir,' the constable informed him, using a nail-bitten finger to indicate a wide pathway between shrubs and trees that led down the near side of the main building. 'If you follow that,' he went on, 'and keep to the right past the pro's shop, that'll bring you out to the eighteenth green, where the bunker is. It's a funny old place to bury a body, isn't it, sir? With all these woods around here, you'd have thought whoever did it could have found a better place than that to hide his victim, wouldn't you?'

'Very likely,' Walsh responded cautiously, glancing at the constable's eager and excited young face. This was probably his first contact with what might be a really serious crime, and you could tell from the animated expression on the boy's face that his mind was racing away, projecting all sorts of scenarios to fit what little he'd been told. No doubt he already had an imaginary list of possible killers, even if he didn't know yet whether the body had been murdered or not.

Walsh gave him a half-smile; maybe he himself had looked as excited as that when he'd been a young copper. 'Very likely,' he repeated absent-mindedly, and then set off towards the path.

This end of the building was quite different in character to the rest of the vast stone-walled, slate-roofed hotel. It had leaded windows and a lower red-tiled roof, and was clearly a much older structure. It was built with massive squared oak timber frames which years of wind and rain had greyed, weathering away the softer wood between the grains and leaving the oak rough and scored. The red bricks that infilled between the timbers were much longer and thinner than modern ones, and they too were worn and pitted by time. One did not need to be an architectural historian to make a pretty shrewd guess that this wing dated from Elizabethan times. It was a beautifully mellow structure, but it was amazing that it had survived so long; clearly the original foundations had been none too solid, and at some time in its history two massive buttresses had been added on one side, in order to keep it all upright. There was a small shrubby garden round it, with a path to an ancient iron-studded oak door.

A little further down the shady path there was another architectural gem. This was a much less substantial building, but about the same age. Its timbers were thinner, and although the roof was now tiled, it needed no stretch of the imagination to visualise it as originally having been a thatched cottage or even a stable. It had been restored and given a modern function: it was now the golf shop. Behind its leaded windows were displays of golf clubs, bags and trolleys.

The path led on under its canopy of branches to a group of garage-like corrugated iron sheds and some piles of rotting grass cuttings: this was obviously where the green-keepers kept their equipment. Further on the path became narrower, winding between high verdant bushes, until all of a sudden Walsh came out into the open and the sunlight. Before him was a broad smooth green, presumably the eighteenth, and beyond that a wide fairway, bordered by yet more trees and shrubs and stretching away into the distance. Here, open to the sun and sheltered from the light cooling breeze, it was humid and warm. Not far away from where he stood were a number of his police force colleagues.

Surprisingly, he felt loath to go over and join them straight away. His mind was still churning over what he had learned at the hospital. The doctors had assured him that the operation had been successful, that his wife, Gwen, was doing fine, but then they had gone on to say that the trouble had been worse than they had expected and that the dubious lumps and bits that they had removed from her were being examined for possible tumours in the pathological laboratory. It was nothing for him to worry about, they had said – but how could he not be worried about something like that? Gwen herself had seemed very wan and pale, her normal vivacity reduced to a tired flicker of a smile of welcome. It was soon pretty obvious that she needed sleep far more than she needed his company, and that he was doing her no favours by denying it to her. His feet had seemed strangely heavy as he'd walked away from her ward, with the spectre of a malignant cancer leering at him over his shoulder.

He ought to go over and politely ask the forensic team what was going on, who was doing what and why, and what had so far been discovered, but the sun on his face and the fresh sweet-smelling air were making him feel light-headed and sleepy. How nice it would be just to sit on the grass, close his eyes and let oblivion erase his worries . . .

He needed to make a positive effort, he told himself, so he walked slowly round the side of the green and went to stand at the top of the deep bunker, where most of the activity was taking place. His shadow darkened the area in which those below were working, causing them to look up in irritation. So he moved further round and crouched down, the better to see what they were doing.

A couple of planks lay on the sand below, and on them knelt two of the scene of crime team, using narrow brushes to clear the particles from round what was quite obviously a dead man's body. The corpse lay on its side with its back to the steepest bunker face, and was now nearly totally exposed, but no attempts were being made to move it. It would not be disturbed until the Home Office pathologist had conducted his initial examination.

It was difficult to judge the age of the man from where Walsh was squatting, though he was clearly an adult. The thick dark hair showed no signs of grey, so he might be somewhere in his twenties or early thirties, probably the latter rather than the former. The face he could not see, but there was a small round blue-tinged wound in the flesh just below the man's left ear; whether that was the cause of death, Walsh had no way of knowing. A wound like that might be made by a small-calibre bullet or even a stab with something as incongruous as a knitting needle. If it were a bullet then its exit point on the unexposed side of the face would be large and torn by splinters of bone being driven outwards. A bullet could hardly have passed through unimpeded. The man wore a thin woollen jumper, herringbone-patterned in grey and white, over a plain white cotton shirt. His blue jeans were worn and well washed, and he wore brown leather sandals on bare feet. That was the sort of casual wear in which a man might lounge about at home, or even wander down to his local pub.

Walsh rubbed at his jaw thoughtfully. It would not have taken very long to dig a hole in the sand of that bunker and to inter the body, for it lay at no great depth; but it would be easily exposed again, as indeed it had. That might suggest that the body had been disposed of in haste. As the young constable at the car-park had observed, there were plenty of places in the thick woods round about where it could have been concealed, even left unburied, with a lot less chance of discovery than where it was. So, why was it buried in this bunker? The answer to that might depend on where the man had died. If it were close by, a woman or a lazy man might have taken the easy option of the soft yellow-white sand, and trusted to luck that it would be a long time before the body was discovered. After all, corpses are heavy and awkward things to move far, without a sledge or wheeled truck.

Walsh turned his head and looked at the hotel on the other side of the green. Where he crouched was in full view of the bar and dining-room downstairs, and all the windows on the first and second floors. Surely no one in their right mind would commit a murder in a place so easily overlooked. Down in the bunker one would be out of sight and one could dig to one's heart's content, but even so, carrying or dragging the body there would have meant taking the risk of being seen.

Perhaps the killer had wanted the body to be found without too much delay. There might be good reasons for that. If there was money to be inherited there could be no probate until the man had been declared officially dead. It would be the same if the man's wife had wanted her freedom without recourse to a lengthy divorce.

Now he was starting to speculate and create imaginary scenarios, just like that young constable at the car-park. What he needed were the answers to some questions. Who was the dead man? Where had he lived? Was he married? How had he died, and when and where? It was pointless running through the checklist yet, but clearly his mind was beginning to function properly, and his lethargy was receding.

He pushed himself to his feet, straightened his back and looked around him with eyes narrowed against the bright sunlight. The whole scene was more clearly defined now. Beyond the back edge of the bunker there was a grassy area of about thirty feet before the shrubs and the trees started again, and just in those shrubs was a small stone building with a round domed roof. He hadn't noticed it before because there was a great deal of ivy doing its best to smother it and engulf it in leafy green. An old summerhouse, presumably. It was in there that the scene of crime team had made a temporary base, for standing in its entrance was the tall, grey-haired figure of the forensic scientist in charge, Dr Richard Packstone.

Walsh now felt ready to start doing the job for which he was paid, and there was no better person than Packstone to brief him on what had been going on. He walked down from the edge of the green, keeping outside the white tape which was lying on the grass, and went over.

'Hello, Sidney. What kept you? Normally we have to do a formula one act to get to the scene of a crime before you do,' Packstone said cheerfully.

'I was at the hospital, seeing Gwen,' Walsh replied reluctantly. He didn't really want to talk about it, but inevitably those who knew about her operation would ask.

Packstone's face lost its smile. 'Has she had the operation yet?'

'Yesterday.'

'Everything all right?'

'Apparently so, but she didn't look too bright and cheerful this morning,' Walsh admitted. His worries about the biopsy tests he would keep to himself.

'Neither would you if you'd had your insides pulled and poked about. She'll hardly be over the effects of the anaesthetic yet. Still, you must be glad that the worst is over. She'll soon pick up,' Packstone replied confidently.

20

'I hope so,' Walsh said with a forced half-smile. Such platitudes were well meant, but they did nothing to ease the sick feeling of worry that was hovering round in the pit of his stomach. It was better to change the subject. 'It looks as though you've been busy. What's been happening?'

Packstone took off his spectacles and polished the lenses vigorously with his handkerchief.

'A woman golfer unearthed the body when she had to play a shot out of the bunker. It must have given her a fair old fright, because she was still shaking like a leaf when we got here. Anyway, the body is that of a local man. The hotel management know him well, apparently. Your two, Reg and Brenda, were here earlier. They've gone off to sort that side of things out. The pathologist will be here, with a bit of luck,' and he looked down at his watch, 'in about half an hour. We've cleared most of the sand away from round the body, but we haven't moved him yet.'

'Any idea how he died, and when?' Walsh asked.

'The wound just below his left jaw-bone looks to me as though it was made by a small-calibre bullet, fired close to. We won't know for sure until we turn him over, but there may be other injuries that we can't yet see. As to when – I don't think he's been dead all that long. Since last night or early this morning, maybe.'

Walsh nodded. 'Was he killed in the bunker, or have you found any signs of his body having been brought here?'

Packstone shook his head and shrugged his shoulders. 'We've no idea where he was killed. We haven't found a gun in the sand, but he might be lying on it. He might have shot himself, but if he did, he certainly didn't bury himself. Someone else must have done that. We've had a good look round the area but we've found no signs of a body being dragged across the grass. It's pretty well overlooked out there, and the nearest cover is these bushes on either side of this summerhouse. We'll have a finger-tip search done later. We won't learn much more until we can examine the body properly, and put his clothing under the microscope.'

There endeth the first briefing, and a pretty brief briefing it was, too, Walsh thought to himself as Packstone walked away, but clues at the site of a murder do not come conveniently typed out in list form, all checked and verified. Hopefully, though,

21

over the next few hours and days the clues might come in fast and furiously. Soon, but not yet, he would start to form the checklist of questions he would want answers to, and near the top of that list would clearly be, how was the body conveyed to this bunker? Packstone and his crew may have found nothing obvious, but if there were tracks, however faint, he had as good a chance of finding them as anyone. At least that would be something constructive to do while he waited for the other members of his serious crime team to come and report to him.

Walsh started his track-hunting at the far side of the eighteenth green, by the hotel's veranda, which was still busily full of the curious and the serious drinkers who preferred to sit at the tables in the sunshine rather than in the comparative gloom of the bar.

The stares of those people Walsh could easily ignore as he paced slowly up and down the green, like a sentry on his beat, with his head bent forward and moving from side to side like a radar scanner. There were no signs of the rents or tears in the turf that a body being dragged along might make. This was a job that would have taxed even the gnarled old Aboriginal tracker who Walsh had spent time with in the Australian deserts many years before, for the ground did not lack signs. There were plenty – spike marks, pitch marks of golf balls, even the heel marks of shoes impressed on wetter days and now dried to a temporary permanence. He soon got the feeling that he was wasting his time. Nevertheless, he dutifully walked all sides of the bunker, to no avail. Then he was back outside the summerhouse again.

It was a funny little building. Even though the roof was domed, the inside was square and surprisingly spacious and light, with several diamond leaded windows set in the thick limestone block walls. There were box seats round three walls, but they didn't look particularly inviting, since they were made of thick granite slabs. The Victorians, or whoever had built the place, must have been pretty stoical to have sat comfortably on those for any length of time, unless they'd brought cushions with them. It was certainly a nice cool place on a hot day. He sat down on a slab seat, reached in his pocket for his tobacco pouch, and proceeded to fill his pipe.

He could, if he wanted, contact and summon the other members of his team by radio, but when he'd lit his pipe and looked outside again, he found that it would not be necessary: two people were walking in a leisurely fashion across the fairway, coming from the hotel. The other senior members of his team were looking for him.

The taller of the two was Detective Sergeant Reginald Finch, six foot one and a bit, lean and fair-haired, in his early thirties, and dressed today in a neat grey suit. He was married to a social worker, was active in supporting a home for handicapped children and had an amateur's interest in most things archaeological or historical.

Beside him walked Detective Constable Brenda Phipps, a much shorter, very pretty young woman in her late twenties, with unruly brown hair, looking particularly slim in a well-tailored pale green linen trouser suit. She looked energetic and fit, the consequence of the frequent unarmed combat training sessions which had made her into one of the constabulary's more adept experts in that field.

Surprisingly, she was also highly skilled in a hobby that required almost no physical prowess, but instead demanded much patience and concentration – restoring to visually perfect condition broken porcelain and ceramic bowls, plates, cups and figurines.

Two apparently incongruous characters, but with himself as a third, they made a pretty good serious crime investigation team.

They'd need to stay pretty good too, for now they were faced with what might well be a taxing new challenge – investigating the death of the man in the bunker on the eighteenth green of the Hasling Abbey golf course.

3

'How is Gwen, Chief?' Brenda Phipps asked, looking rather anxiously at Sidney Walsh's serious face.

'The doctors say the operation went well, and she's fine,' Walsh replied shortly.

'Well, that's good news, boss,' Detective Sergeant Reginald Finch said cheerfully, 'but all she'll want to do for the next few days, probably, is rest and sleep.'

'That's right. She sends her thanks for the flowers, by the way. They looked lovely. She's got masses of them. Her room looks like a stand at the Chelsea Flower Show.' Walsh paused to relight his pipe. 'You've found out who this dead man is, I understand.'

'The dead man's name is Gregory Roger Fitzpatten,' Brenda Phipps announced, stepping back out of the way as a cloud of grey smoke drifted towards her. 'He lives in the Elizabethan wing of the hotel.'

'More precisely, it's a Tudor wing,' Reg Finch corrected. 'It ought to be the Henryan wing, since it's supposed to have been built in the time of Henry VIII, but why it is that you can stick an "an" on the end of some names and not on others, I don't know. Maybe there was nothing made in the reigns of the Henrys, the Charleses and the Williams worth describing.'

'Elizabethan is what the people in the hotel call it, anyway,' Brenda responded promptly.

Reg Finch acknowledged the fact with a slight nod of his head. 'Apparently the Fitzpatten family have owned this place since the monastery was dissolved. When the house was converted into a hotel they kept the original Tudor wing for their own private residence. This Gregory Fitzpatten is a historian and a writer apparently, and he's married to a woman who models clothes. We called and rang the bell, but she's not at home. Well, if she is, she's not answering the door.'

'You can't get into the Elizabethan wing from the hotel, Chief. As Reg says, it's private, and the hotel staff don't have a key,' Brenda explained.

'Who have you actually spoken to?' Walsh asked.

'The assistant manager first, boss,' Reg replied. 'He was the one who came over to identify Fitzpatten, but we only talked to him briefly, because finding this body has put the whole hotel into a bit of a flap. It's full up, you see, and they've got an important golf tournament on. We've also spoken to the golfer who was with the girl who actually found the body. Other than that, all we've done is to set young Arthur Bryant and Alison Knott copying the guest list from the hotel register, and we've found them a room where they can start interviewing those people whose rooms look out over this eighteenth green. Unfortunately that's going to take a long time, since most of the guests are out on the course, watching the golf.'

Walsh pulled on his chin thoughtfully. 'You say the man's married – well, under the circumstances we ought to be a bit concerned about his wife. He obviously didn't sleep at home last night, so if she was there, she should have missed him. He's not been reported missing, has he, Reg?'

Reg Finch shook his head. 'Definitely not, but the wife might be away, she travels a lot, so they said.'

'Even so, since her husband has met with a violent death, we ought to make sure the same thing hasn't happened to his wife. That's sufficient justification for entering this Elizabethan – Tudor wing. If she's not there, then perhaps we'll find something to tell us where she is. Brenda, find out where our friendly locksmith is, and get him here to let us in. What kind of lock is it, Reg?'

'A straightforward Yale. It shouldn't be a problem. Hello! Things are starting to move over there.' He pointed out of the summerhouse towards the bunker. 'It looks as though the pathologist has arrived.'

A group was gathering round where plastic sheeting now covered the body in the sand, and the tall spare figure of Dr Richard Packstone was clearly outlining the situation, with the use of a few gesticulations, to a short, plump, black-suited man,

25

who duly nodded every now and then, but whose small grey eyes were obviously scanning the scene around him, and taking everything in.

Walsh got to his feet quickly. 'You two go up to the Tudor wing, and wait for the locksmith. I'll join you there, when I've heard what the pathologist has to say.'

The pathologist crouched down at the edge of the bunker to study the corpse more closely, then he started talking to a small pocket-sized recording machine.

'The body when found was apparently under several inches of a medium to fine-grained yellowish-white silica sand,' Walsh heard him say. 'By telephone I authorised the removal of that sand prior to my arrival, in order to save time. Right! Now the body is that of a male, aged between twenty-five and thirty-five . . .' He spent the next few minutes describing concisely, yet precisely, what he saw. After that he pushed his fingers into a pair of surgical rubber gloves, and reached forward to lift the body's left arm. It was obviously stiffened, for it moved only slightly, and so it was left to lie with the white fingers still curved upwards in a claw-like fashion. Similarly the neck muscles had locked into solidity, and resisted the half-hearted attempt to turn the man's head.

'Right then,' the pathologist said firmly, standing up and moving to one side. 'You've got all the videos and photos you want, have you, Richard? Good! Now, lay the body bag down there on the front of the sand, and lift him on it. You can turn him over at the same time, so I can see the other side of him.'

It wasn't easy, in the confined space within the bunker, for the four strong members of the scene of crime team to get in the best positions for lifting the corpse, but after a few grunts and groans, that was achieved eventually, and the body was turned over.

The right side of the man's face was in a bit of a mess. It was badly distorted, and caked with congealed sand, but it told a story to the pathologist. 'A small-calibre bullet, fired upwards from under his right jaw,' he muttered loudly enough for Walsh to hear. That was positive enough, but it still left an unanswered question. Had the person committed suicide by blowing his own brain to pieces in what he hoped would be a quick and painless death? If this man had done that, then someone else had subsequently buried him in the sand, and removed the weapon, because there was no sign of it yet in the sand under the body.

26

There was more to be gleaned. The back strap of the left sandal had slipped off the heel: that might mean the body had indeed been dragged, even if there were no obvious tracks. The expensive gold watch on the right wrist had a cracked glass, and there was a long dark green stain on the elbow of the sweater. On the back of the man's blue jeans were several of what appeared to be short white dog-hairs.

Then the body bag was zipped up, and all that remained to be studied was the form and imprint the body had left in the sand.

Reg Finch and Brenda Phipps walked slowly along the woodland path towards the golf shop and the Tudor wing of the hotel.

'We've been lucky so far,' Brenda remarked, turning her head to grin up at her companion. 'Normally in country like this you'd expect the Chief to drag us ten miles or more on our hands and knees following weird tracks through all the thickest bushes and brambly hedges he can find.'

'Don't speak too soon. He might do that later on,' Reg replied with a shrug of his broad shoulders. 'He's got other things on his mind at the moment. He's worried about Gwen. You could see that.'

'Why should he worry? The operation's been done and Gwen's fine. There was more to worry about yesterday than there is today.'

'He'll have different worries now. Margaret thinks there may have been more behind that operation than the boss has told us,' Reg said seriously. Margaret was Reg's wife, and a social worker with a nursing background, so her views carried weight.

'Such as?' Brenda asked.

'Growths – tumours – things that might be malignant. They won't know until they've done a biopsy. He'll be more worried about that than he was about the operation. I would be if I were him.'

'Worrying doesn't do any good. She'll be all right. She's in the right place. She won't get better medical care anywhere than she will at Addenbrooke's,' Brenda said with all the confidence of someone who was as fit as a fiddle, and to whom any kind of illness was almost unknown.

27

They were nearing the Tudor wing now, where a thick laurel hedge enclosed and made private a small rear garden. A narrow path gave access to what was now the apartment's front door but in earlier times had probably been a servants' entrance. There was a small white van parked on the path outside, and that its engine had been left running was evidenced by the puffs of grey-white smoke that curled from the end of its rusty exhaust pipe. The iron-studded dark oak front door of the Tudor wing, set in the ancient flat red bricks and arched by white-flowered climbing roses, stood wide open.

'Good! Someone's home,' Reg exclaimed, lengthening his stride and heading down the narrow pathway. He went in through the doorway into a cool stone-flagged hallway.

'Hello there!' he called out loudly, but then he was swung round sharply as Brenda grabbed his coat sleeve and yanked on it.

'Hold on, Reg,' she whispered loudly and excitedly. 'Look at that door frame. Someone's used a jemmy on it. See there.' She pointed to some raw splintering of the wood near the lock.

Reg's face became frowningly serious, and wary. He went cautiously through the hall into the room opposite. Two men were in there, and both had their faces turned towards the doorway and the newcomers, but whether they expressed surprise or annoyance at the arrival of visitors was not clear – both faces were just then being finally concealed under pulled-down stocking-top masks. The taller of the two men was having some problems with his. He'd yanked the material down so hastily that the eye holes were down to the same level as his nose, and he was finding it difficult to readjust the thing, particularly since he was wearing gloves and holding a jemmy in his right hand. Nevertheless, as soon as vision was restored to one eye, he started moving towards the door – and Reg – with the jemmy raised threateningly.

That jemmy was a formidable weapon; the claw end of the loop shone where it had been ground to a sharp edge, and it was obviously heavy. A blow from that could be bone-shattering, and lethal.

Plain-clothed British CID officers do not normally carry batons and cans of CS gas; faced with an unexpected physical encounter, they have to make do as best they can. Reg Finch had an instinctive desire to turn round and run, but he didn't do that. It wasn't a matter of male pride, it was common sense. Running was probably the worst thing he could do, for there was no way he could ward off a blow if he was facing in the wrong direction. He forced himself to move forward, to go on to the attack himself. He would have to rely on his own strength, reactions and training, to keep himself out of serious trouble.

There were vital split-second decisions to be made as he advanced. He raised his left arm with the fingers outstretched, ready to grasp the wrist holding the jemmy, and with his right hand there was just time enough to reach out and flick rather than throw a small mahogany table at the oncoming man. It did not impede him, but it sufficed to distract him and spoil the timing of the blow aimed at Reg's head. Reg grasped the wrist of the hand with the jemmy, then twisted and turned his body, and tried to toss the man over his shoulder. That was fine, but things started to go wrong. His own feet got caught up in the legs of the mahogany table, nearly tripping him, so the man merely ended up on Reg's back; and while there he hooked his left arm round Reg's throat and proceeded to try and break his neck with vicious backward tugs, while at the same time struggling to free his jemmy-holding wrist. Reg started to get anxious, this contest was following no ordered and safe police training routine. He bent forward to try and shake the man off that way, but that didn't work, so he set his legs staggering forward in as much of a charge as he could manage, and tried to smash his opponent's head against the wall. That succeeded to some degree since, when they both collapsed into an untidy heap, Reg heard the jemmy fall to the floor. At least now the odds were evened to one unarmed man against another. Reg tried for an arm lock, but his opponent writhed and wriggled so much that every time he got a grip, it was instantly broken. Unfortunately, his opponent was trying to do much the same sort of thing to him, so he was spending as much time getting himself out of trouble as he was getting the other into it. So it was that the battle degenerated into a rolling maul of short vicious punches and fingers gouging at eyes and throats.

Brenda Phipps could give him no aid, for she was fully occupied. The shorter man was stocky and powerfully built, and as she entered the room she found him charging at her also with a weapon in his hand. It was not a sharpened jemmy, but an

29

aerosol tin of spray paint, with which he had previously been creating graffiti of dubious artistic merit on the apartment's walls. Such an instrument may not have been fearsomely lethal, but a squirt of its contents in the face would have been temporarily blinding. Brenda, however, had a weapon of her own. She carried a variety of useful bits and pieces in a small brown leather shoulder bag, and that, swung round flail-like in a manner of which Lady Thatcher herself might well have approved, sufficed to deflect the squirt of black paint away from her eyes, and harmlessly down the front of her smart green trouser-suit jacket. That was more than enough to release the tigress in Brenda. This situation of a man coming at her with arm raised was simple routine stuff on the unarmed combat courses at which she excelled. She grasped the man's upraised arm with both her hands, twisted forward, bent her back, heaved, and sent him flying over her shoulders to the floor. She did not, however, release her grip; instead she twisted his wrist and bent the fingers of his hand right back and pulled, at the same time kicking her heel into the man's armpit. When she straightened her leg the man screamed with agony as his shoulder was pulled out of its joint. That was quite enough for him. He gave up, and confined his aggressive efforts to trying to gain sympathy by making whimpering little groans.

Brenda now had time to see how Reg was getting on. That battle was still being energetically fought. They were well matched in physique and strength, and were about even on points. Each would occasionally get on top, but then a renewed effort from the other would result in the tables being turned again.

Brenda's opponent seemed to be subdued and helpless, but appearances could be deceptive, so when she went to Reg's aid she took him with her. She dragged him along by his twisted arm, ignoring his even louder screams of pain, then kicked Reg's adversary as hard as she could in the groin. She missed that area, but the lower stomach was nearly as good, for it sufficed to double the man up and render him sufficiently *hors de combat* for Reg to scramble shakily to his feet.

'There's a pair of handcuffs in my bag,' Brenda panted out breathlessly. 'Get them on your man first. This one's no trouble.'

Reg, however, used his own set of handcuffs to secure his erstwhile opponent's wrists behind his back, before delving into Brenda's bag for the other pair to render her man even more helpless than he already was.

Brenda breathed a long sigh of relief. 'That was exciting while it lasted, wasn't it?' she exclaimed with the offhandedness of one who had been well in control of her situation from start to finish.

'Like hell it was,' Reg Finch growled angrily, as he straightened his tie and then ran his fingers through his tousled overlong fair hair. He was shaken, bruised and battered, and his limbs felt as if they had no strength left in them. Yet his mind was functioning properly.

'See if your radio is still working, Brenda,' he said gruffly, 'and call an ambulance. Your man's shoulder's out of joint, and the kick you gave this one has probably burst his guts. They'll probably complain to the Police Complaints Board that we've used an excessive amount of force anyway, but we don't want either of them dying on us. That'll only make things worse. We'd better have a couple of uniformed men here as escorts too.'

He rubbed at the muscles at the back of his neck while glancing around the room. The ceiling was coved and decoratively plastered with leafy garlands and Tudor roses. Its height was about normal for a modern house, but it seemed low, because of the spaciousness of the room. It was dim in there too, in spite of there being two wide leaded windows, but that was because the walls were all lined with an oak linenfold panelling much darkened by age, except where there was a broad carved stone fireplace which was nearly big enough to roast the proverbial ox. It was a beautiful room, with history simply oozing from every nook and cranny, and one in which a person might immediately feel relaxed and at home, were it not in such a dreadful mess. Cushions, pictures, books and papers lay in an untidy heap in the centre of the room.

This, presumably, was the task that their two defeated antagonists had been undertaking when he and Brenda had arrived to interrupt them. Now his eyes had become more accustomed to the light he could see that paint had been sprayed on that beautiful oak panelling. It was dark paint, which was why he hadn't noticed it before. It wasn't wild haphazard graffiti; those shapes formed the letters N and F several times over. Reg frowned and his weary face now became even more serious.

31

'NF' usually meant 'National Front', those tough and uncompromising individuals whose philosophies of life were akin to those of Germany's Nazi party of the 1930s, when violence was a normal political expedient.

Having used her radio to summon assistance, Brenda remembered the reason why the two of them had come to the Tudor wing: to ascertain the whereabouts of the wife of the man found dead in the bunker, and to discover whether her life, too, had been ended abruptly. The confusion of battle had obviously put it out of Reg's mind.

'I'll check upstairs. You look after these two for a minute,' she said abruptly, and went off to explore the other rooms of the apartment.

One door from the hallway was to a smallish but well-fitted modern kitchen; another opened into an elegant period dining-room which, like the sitting-room, was panelled in oak. On a large sideboard stood several large porcelain bowls that glowed with bright and vivid colours, but Brenda resisted the temptation to stop and examine them just then. Hopefully there would be time to do that later. The fourth door from the hall was smaller than the others, a mere cupboard perhaps, but there was no way of verifying that since it was fitted with a very modern Yale lock. When she turned the old-fashioned handle and pushed, the door budged not an inch. So she left it, and hurried up the stairs to the floor above, failing to appreciate the historic authenticity of the black-painted wooden frames which were exposed on the half-landing, or that the white-painted plaster between reflected the light and made it much brighter there than in the rooms downstairs.

The largest of the upper rooms had an old four-poster bed with modern material draping the canopy. Next to that was an ultra-modern tiled bathroom and two smaller bedrooms. Brenda looked in the wardrobes and cupboards and under the beds, but there was no other occupant, dead or alive, or any of the mayhem that had been created in the sitting-room. Her duty done, she went downstairs intending to make time for a quick look at those brightly coloured bowls in the dining-room. Chinese, hand-painted and oldish, well, nineteenth-century at least, that had been her impression from a distance. It would be nice to see if she was right . . . but it was not to be. Sidney Walsh was standing in the hallway.

32

'Hello, Chief,' she exclaimed brightly. 'What did the pathologist have to say?'

'Not a great deal that we couldn't already see for ourselves, but the man was shot in the head, and there was no pistol lying about. Now, I hope you're not going to tell me our locksmith made a mess like that,' he said, pointing to the splintered wood of the door post where the lock socket had been torn away from the frame. 'And what on earth have you been doing to your clothes?' he went on, looking down at the pale green jacket of her trouser suit, now liberally sprayed with black paint.

Brenda grimaced. 'I rather got in the way of a tin of aerosol paint, didn't I? It's dry now, but it'll never come off. That's another outfit ruined in the line of duty. If this keeps up I'll be buying all my clothes from the Oxfam shop. No, our tame locksmith didn't do this, he hasn't arrived, and he won't now, because I rang him to say there wasn't a panic any more. The door was like this when we got here, and we disturbed a couple of toughs trying to wreck the place.'

'Did you now? That's very interesting. Who are they? Have they said what they were up to?'

Brenda shrugged. 'They weren't in the mood for a cosy chat when I last saw them. I've just been making sure Mrs Fitzpatten's not lying dead in the house somewhere, and she's not.'

'Well, that's one good thing then,' Walsh commented as he walked through into the sitting-room.

One quick glance round the room sufficed to tell the story.

The two men lay uncomfortably on their sides on the floor, both still wearing their stocking masks. The pile of cushions, broken drawers, books and papers in the middle of the room seemed to suggest that those two men had intended to start a fire. With the owner of the place dead in suspicious circumstances it did not take much intelligence to work out that a fire here might be intended to destroy some vital evidence, but the question as to why such a fire hadn't been created earlier, since Fitzpatten had obviously been dead for some time, was one to which he would have liked an answer.

He tried to get one by questioning the two men, but that turned out to be a futile exercise. Not for the first time in his professional career, he found himself wishing that the methods of the old-time Catholic Inquisitors were legally available for him to use, but the pampered society of the modern day liked to wallow in the dubious mire of moral self-righteousness by banning the judicious use of a little bit of pain in the quest for truth. A flame to the soles of bare feet, a bit of thumb-screwing or a stretch on the rack might have achieved useful answers, instead of the flow of foul language and abusive epithets that was remarkable only for the sheer range and variety achieved before the need arose to resort to repetition. Experienced police officers are frequently exposed to such language, and are hardly likely to admire an extended tirade, but words that were new engendered curiosity.

'What on earth's a . . . oh well, never mind,' Brenda exclaimed, interrupting Walsh as he switched from the cajoling 'You're in big trouble, but we'll help you if you help us', interrogation ploy, to the one that lists all the possible serious charges that might be made, and the resultant lengths of the prison sentences likely, if co-operation was not forthcoming.

He might as well have saved his breath. These two had clearly heard it all before, and had no intention of co-operating, so Walsh ended up none the wiser as to who they were and why they were there. Rummaging through the men's pockets produced no useful information either.

'Ask HQ to run a vehicle check on their van, Brenda,' he asked, hopeful that he might learn something from that. He did: the van had been stolen earlier that morning in North London.

Then the ambulance and police reinforcements arrived to escort the two toughs away for medical treatment and subsequent close confinement in a cell. Fingerprints and reference to the national register of known criminals would, no doubt, identify them in time.

Reg Finch had not involved himself with the interrogation. His head still ached, so he had set about the physically and mentally undemanding task of sorting through the untidy mess of papers and debris in the middle of the room.

'Have you found anything useful, Reg?' Walsh asked him.

'I don't know, yet,' Reg replied from where he sat in a comfortable armchair, the cushions of which he had found and replaced. 'The fellow was definitely a writer, there are a few letters here from a literary agent and another from a publisher. I've also found some bank statements. He wasn't short of a bob or two.'

'Have you seen signs of a fight under this mess?'

'No, only where Brenda and I had our confrontation with those two thugs. Whether any of this mess was here before those two arrived, I can't tell.' He reached down to put some papers into neat piles on the floor at his feet. 'I'm only skipping through these, roughly sorting them out. We'll have to go through them again later, but what I'm really looking for is an appointments book, or a diary of some sort, that might tell us where Mrs Fitzpatten is.'

Walsh nodded. 'You carry on, then. We'll get Forensic to examine this area of the carpet when we've tidied up a bit more. I think it's unlikely that the man was killed in that sand bunker, so possibly he was killed here in his own home.'

To speed the tidying process Walsh himself bent down to pick up a picture. The glass in the ornate frame was cracked but not splintered, and beneath it was a lovely little water-colour painting of a thatched croft cottage, with grass and meadow flowers stretching out into a distant hazy countryside. In the foreground there was a stream, and a woman in period clothing crossing a plank bridge with a basket in her hand. He walked over to the window where the light was better. This had been painted by a real artist, with such a delicacy of brush stroke that he felt quite envious. Some years ago he'd tentatively taken up painting as a hobby, and had thoroughly enjoyed the little free time he'd been able to devote to it. He leaned it safely against the wall, out of harm's way, and picked up another. This was a modern impressionist picture, but apart from there being something stimulating about the vividness of the colours, it left him coldly indifferent.

Brenda Phipps seemed more interested in the broken drawers of the antique and valuable bureau. The walnut-veneered fronts had survived the rough handling but the sides and the bottoms were now what most people would consider as firewood; yet she knew that each piece could be carefully glued and, if clamped tightly together, they could eventually, with patience, be made so whole again that only an experienced craftsman might realise that they had ever been damaged. It was a task she would be quite happy to undertake, if the bureau were hers. However, she carefully put all the pieces to one side, where careless feet would not inflict further damage. She then picked up a photograph album, sat down on the spacious settee, and proceeded to turn the pages. The early pictures were mostly of children and parents of the fifties, perhaps sixties, but after a while she was able to recognise the features of a growing youth who was common to most prints. He was a startlingly attractive young man: tall and broad-shouldered, with dark hair and big laughing eyes, and a slightly twisted smile that gave even her heart a little flutter. The pictures became those of college days, and recognisable places. A punt on the river Cam by King's, a view of the Bridge of Sighs in St John's, cricket, rugby, rowing and golf. The golf was not here at Hasling Abbey, but on the open chalkland of the Cambridge Gog Magog course. Then there was a photograph of someone with the handsome young man who she actually recognised: a short, tubby, nearly bald man who was smiling cheerfully out of the glossy print.

'Hey, Chief,' she called out. 'Here's a picture of Fitzpatten with old Professor Hughes. That is the courtyard of Downing College, isn't it?'

Walsh looked over her shoulder. 'Yes, that's right. That's Professor Hughes. Maybe Fitzpatten was an undergrad there. There's still nothing about Mrs Fitzpatten yet, though. That's who we've got to talk to first. Keep looking.'

It might be that in this family the wife kept her private papers in a different room, perhaps in the bedroom, or dining-room, but before he went to explore upstairs he decided to go outside and smoke a pipe. It had become unacceptable behaviour nowadays, to smoke in someone else's house, but outside in the fresh air no one could complain. Well, that wasn't really true, they could and did complain. Some anti-smokers were getting as fanatical as any fundamentalist religious zealot.

As he walked out of the front door with those thoughts in his mind, he quite literally bumped into one of the most beautiful women he'd ever seen in his life.

'I'm so sorry,' he said as he hurriedly took a step back, there to stand in gawky stillness while his eyes surveyed the vision before him.

Her face was more of an oval than simply round and its features were near perfect. A snubbily pert nose, exquisitely shaped lips, a flawless complexion and large green eyes – emerald green – with tiny golden flecks in the irises. You could use a million different words to describe them, but only beautiful would really do.

36

Those eyes were looking straight into his own, and they now bore an expression that was disconcertingly cool, dispassionate and disinterested, much as an enthroned and bejewelled queen might gaze down at a mere suppliant peasant. It wasn't just her eyes, her whole face drew a viewer's gaze and held it, like some wonderful painting in which there was so much exquisitely executed detail to be noted, admired and absorbed that it was almost impossible to look away. That face, clearly, was accustomed to being stared at in such a way, but it would permit such an intensive study only for a certain period of time. Those delicate fair eyebrows eventually arched and rose into an inquisitorial expression that clearly indicated that the time so graciously allowed for adoration was at an end.

'Perhaps you would now be kind enough to carry my case into the hall?' she asked in a soft, well-modulated, girlish voice that somehow seemed to contain the faint tinkling of tiny crystal bells. At the same time the eyes switched on a beseeching expression, which contained a broad hint that on completion of the task there might follow a look of eternal gratitude and even other, more intimate, promises.

That brought Walsh back down to earth with a thud. His face reddened with the realisation that he'd been staring at her like a gormless callow youth. Beautiful women, and many who fell into a lower classification of attractiveness, often assumed that all the men who gazed at them admiringly became mindless fawning morons who would slavishly take on any task that they were bid. Well, he, Walsh, had been out in the big wide world a long time, and he was not one of that ilk. Not now that he was older and wiser. So he frowned and tried to look sternly impassive. 'And who might you be?' he asked gruffly.

The eyebrows of the beautiful face rose even higher and a slight smile creased round the perfect lips. Perhaps she was also used to older men being frightened of acting like callow youths.

'I'm Lynda Fitzpatten, of course,' she tinkled melodically. 'I'm the lady of this house, and I'd like to go inside, if you please. I see no reason why you should keep me standing at my own front door.'

Walsh stepped back to allow her to walk, or float, gracefully past him. Now he could survey the rest of her. She was fair-haired and slender in a white lacy blouse and slacks of a subtle shade of pink, both of which had been exquisitely and expensively tailored to display the perfection of the figure beneath.

'Mrs Fitzpatten? I've some bad news for you, I'm afraid,' Walsh called after her as he grabbed the suitcase from the path and hurried back into the hallway.

'Yes, I can see you have,' Mrs Lynda Fitzpatten murmured as her gaze roamed over her disordered sitting-room. She must have been surprised and shocked at finding her home occupied by strangers and in such a state, but the only facial signs she gave of having such emotions were a hardening of her jaw muscles and a slight pursing of her lips. 'It must have been a pretty wild party. What a pity about the bureau, I rather liked that, and my sheepskin rug from the fireplace? Is that ruined too? What a shame.'

Brenda Phipps stood up as the newcomer crossed the room, and found herself being eyed inquisitively from head to toe.

'You poor thing,' Mrs Fitzpatten exclaimed icily. 'Those trouser suits went out of fashion years ago, but you're using it for the right thing though, darling,' she went on, pointing at the paint sprayed on Brenda's jacket, 'if your idea of fun is doing up old cars. Are you one of Gregory's girls? I must say you don't look his type, but any port in a storm, they say, don't they? Well, where is he then? Where is Gregory? Sleeping it off upstairs?'

'Your husband, Mrs Fitzpatten, I'm afraid, is dead,' Walsh said quietly from where he stood by the door.

'Oh yes!' she exclaimed angrily, turning to face him with eyes blazing. 'He's gone out and shot himself, I suppose? Pull the other leg, do. Dead drunk more likely.'

'Mrs Fitzpatten, I am a police officer, and what I say is, unfortunately, true,' Walsh said calmly, drawing out his warrant identification card from his pocket and holding it out for her to see. 'We're all police officers. Cambridgeshire Constabulary, Criminal Investigation Department. Your husband's body was found this morning, and he'd been shot in the head.'

Still disbelieving, the woman took the warrant card from Walsh's hand, and glanced from the photograph on it to Walsh's face, then back down again to the official wording.

Slowly an expression of appalled horror came on her face, and, even as the tears began to well from her emerald green eyes, her body crumpled in the middle and she sank to the floor in a dead faint. Walsh just managed to grab her shoulders before her head hit the carpet. She was surprisingly heavy, for one who looked so willowy and frail.

'Well, you didn't handle that very diplomatically, did you, Chief?' Brenda Phipps admonished, as she knelt down to check the woman's pulse at the base of the neck.

Walsh shrugged phlegmatically. 'She didn't want to listen, did she? Call for a doctor to come and administer to her, will you, Brenda? You'd better stay here with her until he comes. We'd better not touch anything else. If there's a rug missing then maybe Fitzpatten was killed here, in this room. We'll get Richard Packstone and his crew to check this place over. Come on, Reg, we'll go and tell him, and then I want to talk to the manager of this hotel. It seems a funny old set-up here, maybe he can tell us what it's all about.'

4

'I won't keep you a moment,' said the middle-aged and portly hotel manager, whose name was Houghton. There was sweat on his brow and he was clearly flustered as he straightened his bow tie with one nervous hand while at the same time taking a quick look at the watch on the other wrist. 'If you'd just take a seat in my office, I'll be back in a jiff. We're in the middle of lunch, and we're full to busting. If we're going to get problems, now is the time.'

The office was windowless and small. A desk and three chairs sufficed to fill it, yet there was room for a Busy Lizzy among the files on a narrow shelf and, judging by the number of flowers on it, it thrived under artificial light. There was also a large ashtray on the manager's desk that had been well used by a cigarette smoker, so Walsh felt no compunction about lighting his pipe.

'Ever eaten here, Reg?' he asked as he sat down on one of the visitors' chairs.

'No, but I've heard people say it's not bad,' Reg replied, rubbing tentatively at a shoulder still sore from the battering he'd taken earlier. Other aches were working their way to the surface.

When the manager came back in he sat down at his desk and gave a long drawn-out sigh. 'It's been one hell of a morning. I don't want another like it, thank you very much. Sudden deaths, and hordes of policemen all over the place, if you'll forgive me for saying so, do the reputations of hotels no good at all, especially when they make the eighteenth green a complete no-go area. I've had the company running the golf tournament going on at me as though it was all my fault. I've told them they'll just have to play it over seventeen holes this year. They've got no other choice, have they? Still, there's no good crying over spilt milk. Now, you want to talk to me about Gregory Fitzpatten, I suppose.'

'That's right, but fill us in on some background first. How does it come about that he can live in a wing of this hotel?' Walsh asked.

'That's easy. The Fitzpattens owned this place for donkeys' years. The men were Sir Fitzpattens once, but that died out. I don't know why. Anyway, what with death duties and a taste for good living, this one's dad and the one before him didn't have money to waste on basic repairs, so the house was falling to pieces. Then someone suggested to him that he'd still got enough land left to build a golf course, and the house might make a money-spinning hotel, like Gleneagles up in Scotland. He wasn't over-keen at first, apparently, but he chewed it over, put the idea about among his friends, and finally got an insurance company interested. So, a company was set up, and the project went ahead, with himself as one of the shareholders. It must have been a big decision for him, giving up the ancestral home, but things didn't turn out so bad. The Elizabethan wing didn't really fit in with the architect's plans for the hotel conversion. They couldn't alter floor levels and ceiling heights, or put in bigger windows, because it was a listed building, and they couldn't knock it down either, which is what they would rather have done. Anyway, they decided that Fitzpatten could keep that bit for himself as a private wing, provided he paid for the restoration. Which is what he did, although he did most of the internal work himself, under the supervision of the County Architect's department. He made a good job of it too. He was a nice old boy, but he died the year after I first came here. So, young Gregory Fitzpatten, he was twenty-something then, just finished getting his degree at Cambridge, he inherited his old man's hotel shares. The board gave him a non-executive director's seat out of respect for the old man, and he came to live in the Elizabethan wing. He was no problem, really, although I never did like the fellow. He was young then, you see, and cocky. His idea was that life was all fun and games, like one enormous Rag Week. He used the hotel dining-room and bar fairly frequently, and although he never exactly got roaring drunk, when he'd had one or two he'd quite often get into heated arguments with some of the guests. Which didn't go down well, I can tell you.'

41

Houghton stopped talking for a moment as one of his staff came in with a tray containing a coffee pot and some cups. 'Thanks,' he said, giving the waitress an appreciative nod. 'You'll both join me, won't you? How do you like it? Black? White? Help yourselves to sugar.'

'White, thanks. Go on. What else can you tell us about the dead man? Do you know whether he had any enemies, or why anyone might want to kill him?' Walsh asked.

Houghton's face twitched and scowled. 'Ah! That's the hundred thousand dollar question, isn't it? Our Gregory's morals left a lot to be desired where women were concerned. It didn't matter to him whether they were married or single, young or old, or what they looked like. There won't be many fellows crying themselves to sleep when they learn his chips have been cashed in. Well, he'd got everything going for him, hadn't he? Brains, a fancy bit of an ancestral home, sporty cars, as well as a body like Tarzan and the looks to go with it. Women couldn't resist him when he put on the old "come hither". Mind you, his dad was a bit like that too, from all accounts, so it probably runs in the family. We all hoped he might settle down when he married Lynda, but I suppose the style of life he still led threw too many juicy temptations in his way.'

'What was his style of life, then?' Reg Finch asked.

'Well, he was often in London, hanging around in the places where the people from the media go, trying to hobnob with the television producers. That was his ambition, to get in front of the cameras and become a famous celebrity. He wrote history books, you see. I don't know how good they are, because they're not the kind of thing I read, but he tried really hard to get them televised as a series, with himself as the presenter, of course. He had visions of being another Magnus Magnusson or a David Attenborough. The last I heard he was setting out to do something really controversial, but just what that was I don't know. He could have been a pretty good golfer if he'd put his mind to it. He had a handicap of six or seven, and never a minute spent practising.'

'I got the impression from his wife that he used to throw some pretty wild parties,' Walsh prompted.

'At times. He'd have groups of his London cronies come up, or people he knew in Cambridge from his university days. He'd

42

wine them and dine them in the hotel here, then they'd all go back to his place to have their orgy or rave.'

'So you think there are a few husbands about who might have had violent feelings towards Fitzpatten, do you?' Walsh found himself studying the manager's plump white face more intently than he had before. The extra-marital relationships of the unfaithful generally stirred fiery passions in those who felt they had been wronged, and passions like that could seethe and smoulder until the light breeze of opportunity suddenly fanned them into a roaring furnace. Even the mildest of persons might well end up doing something they'd live to regret.

Houghton paused. 'Not just husbands. Fitzpatten had a weakness for girls as well as women, so I understand from gossip. There might be a few outraged dads kicking about as well.'

'That's a pretty positive statement, Mr Houghton. What I'd like from you are some specific instances of Fitzpatten's womanising, in the strictest confidence, of course,' Walsh said coaxingly.

Houghton's lips, however, came together stubbornly, and he shook his head as he looked down at his hands.

'Come, come, Mr Houghton. You've had this rampant womaniser on the premises for nigh on ten years. You must know a hell of a lot about his private life, whether it's real or gossip. Come on, you made the accusations, now back them up,' Walsh demanded.

Again Houghton shook his head. 'I've only told you what I've heard people say – besides, I don't live on the premises. I live in the village.'

'You don't live on the premises? I thought it was standard practice for hotel managers. Isn't there an apartment here for you?'

'Well, yes. We lived in it for a couple of years when we first came here, but it's too poky. The village is much more convenient for the schools and shops,' Houghton explained reluctantly.

'"We"? "Schools"? So you're married, and with children. How old are they? Boys or girls?' Reg Finch asked, looking up from the notebook over which his pencil was poised.

'Yes, of course I'm married, and we've two children. Jo, she's fifteen, and Tristan, he's twelve, but I don't know what the hell that's got to do with it,' Houghton protested.

43

'We're just checking whether your memory is still working. It seems you can remember your children's names, but when it comes to the names of the women Fitzpatten is supposed to have had affairs with these last ten years, your mind goes completely blank. That sounds a bit strange, doesn't it?' Reg questioned remorselessly.

'No, it isn't,' Houghton said, blinking desperately. 'I hear lots of gossip, about all sorts of people. If I remembered everything, I'd have a mind like an encyclopaedia. My brain can't take it all in. I get the gist of what's said, but the details go in one ear and out the other.'

It was clearly pointless trying to pursue that particular aspect further at the present time.

'All right. What can you tell us about Mrs Fitzpatten?' Walsh demanded calmly.

'Lynda? You must have seen her face dozens of times in the television adverts and glossy magazines.' Houghton seemed relieved to have the subject matter of the conversation changed. 'Beautiful, isn't she? She and he made a right pair. She could give him as good as she got when it came to sleeping around, but in her case she was only interested in men with money or influence. When she crooked her little finger, believe me, they came running, unless there was something wrong with their hormones. So they say.'

'"So they say." Any instances, or is that just gossip too?' Reg Finch asked with a supercilious look on his face.

Houghton shrugged his shoulders, and nodded.

'What time did you leave here last night? Did you see anything out of the ordinary? Or can't you remember that either?' Walsh enquired grimly.

'Of course I can. I went off at about twenty past nine, when all the night staff had turned up, but I didn't see anything unusual. I can't tell you whether Fitzpatten was around or not. His car wasn't where he normally parks it, but that's because it's in the garage for repair, and I don't know what they've lent him instead.'

'What does he usually drive?' Reg Finch wanted to know.

'A Jaguar coupé, metallic green – two years or so old. He usually parks in the far corner of the car-park, close to his place.'

'We'll need to talk to your night staff when they come on duty. I'd appreciate you giving us a list of their names and job titles before they get here,' Walsh requested.

Houghton seemed only too willing to oblige, and be helpful – now.

'No problem there, but I'll tell you who you ought to have a word with, and that's Andy Myres, he's our resident professional. He lives in the flat over the golf shop, just down from the Elizabethan wing. He might easily have seen something. Then there's Grant Finlay, the head green-keeper. He's usually the last person out on the course at night, and the first in the mornings. He's getting on a bit but he doesn't miss much of what goes on out on the golf course, or anywhere else, for that matter.'

'Well, thanks for the coffee, Mr Houghton,' Walsh said as he got up to leave. 'We may need to talk to you again.'

'Any time,' the manager replied confidently. 'If your people are going to be interviewing more of our guests, I'd appreciate it if they could be as unobtrusive as possible.'

'They will be,' Walsh acknowledged, as he closed the office door behind him.

'Presumably Houghton's wife was one of Fitzpatten's early victims,' Reg Finch suggested with a grin.

'I think you're probably right. We'll sort all that out later. We're bound to find some gossip somewhere who'll enjoy spilling the beans,' Walsh replied. 'In the meantime it might be a good idea if you had a word with this golf professional, Myres. If he lives over the golf shop he may have seen something, or heard the sound of a shot last night. I want to go and see how Forensic are doing. I'll meet you back at Fitzpatten's place, later.'

Reg Finch looked round the inside of the golf shop with undisguised interest. It was one big open area, with the wall timbers left exposed and the rough brickwork neatly pointed up with a whitish lime-based mortar. The whole restoration had been expertly done, with a sympathetic understanding of the period in which it had been built, and that was pleasing to Reg. Here was a fine example of a Tudor building, probably looking much as it might have done when it was first constructed, downstairs at least. The interior was surprisingly cool, compared with the warmth outside, but perhaps that was partly due to the stone-flagged floor.

'They tell me it probably started off as a row of workers' cottages,' Andy Myres said offhandedly. 'It's not as solidly built as the main house, but even so, it hasn't done badly, has it? I'm not much into history and that sort of thing, but it serves my purpose very nicely, although I do get a lot of people coming here just to see the place, rather than buy anything. Maybe I ought to charge an admission fee. Are you a golfer, sergeant? I've got some nice matched sets of clubs to get you started, if you're interested. They're second-hand but they're in good condition, and they're cheap. You can spread your payments over six months too, if you like.'

'No thanks. I do have some clubs, but I haven't used them for years. I don't get the time,' Reg said reluctantly. He'd played a bit when he'd been younger, and enjoyed the fresh air and the exercise, and the rare occasions when he'd hit the ball cleanly and sent it roughly where he'd wanted it to go, but that hadn't happened often enough for the golf bug to bite deep into his system.

Myres was an interesting-looking character. He was of medium height, broad-shouldered and with a thick mop of jet black hair that started only an inch or so above his equally black and slanted eyebrows. His face was pinched and gaunt, and with his hooked beak of a nose he'd need little make-up to play the part of Mephistopheles or the devil incarnate. However, he also had a rather vacuous expression in his soft brown eyes, which might suggest to the unkind that he was a Jekyll and Hyde character. The backs of the man's hands were certainly unusually hairy.

'You live over the shop here, I believe,' Reg went on to say, putting such impressions to the back of his mind.

'That's right,' Myres confirmed pleasantly. 'It's been made into a nice little self-contained flat. Ideal for a bachelor golf freak like me. It's funny how life goes, isn't it? When I was eight or nine I wanted to be a palaeontologist, and spend my life digging up dinosaur bones. Then when I was ten, I had one round on the pitch and putt course in Hunstanton, and that was me hooked for life. All I ever wanted to do after that was to drop the little white ball in the hole. My school work went to pot, because as soon as the bell went for the end of lessons, I'd be off on my bike to somewhere grassy, and I'd chip chip chip and putt putt putt, until it was time to go to bed. I had no time for anything else, but

46

that didn't bother me, not then. By the time I discovered what women were for, it was too late. I was much too set in my ways for marriage. They'd have been grass widows even before they'd finished walking down the aisle, and they knew it. Golf's my life, that's all there is to it.'

He was fortunate if he accepted things as simply as that. With a face like his, even the kindest and most understanding of people might be put off from close friendship. It would not be surprising if this man were a little bitter and withdrawn from real life, even if he didn't show it outwardly.

'It's nice to have a job doing something you like,' Reg said, rather impatiently. He'd not come here to listen to someone's life story or to psychoanalyse a social misfit. 'This place is only a stone's throw from where the Fitzpattens live. Did you see him last night? Or did you see anyone going to or from his apartment?'

'I didn't see him in the bar when I was doing my social bit, meeting club members and listening to their stories about where they'd sliced this shot, or pulled that one, and the putts that just would not go in the hole. That's when I suggest that their stance or their grip might need a bit of adjustment, and that a few lessons with me might knock ten strokes off their handicaps. That's my living. You get the odd bore who can't swing the same twice running, but by and large I enjoy it, because they do play better afterwards, until their bad habits creep back again.'

'Was he at home last night, do you know?'

'I didn't see any signs of life in his place when I went to the bar, as far as I recall, and his car wasn't where he normally parks it. So perhaps he was out. I don't know. I didn't come back that way. It was a nice evening, so I went for a stroll down the first fairway, cut across the seventh and the ninth, and came back down the eighteenth. There were a few people about, but I can't tell you who they were. Hotel guests most likely.'

'Did you see or hear anything suspicious anywhere? Anything out of the ordinary? Anything that might have sounded like a gun shot?'

'I can't say as I did, I'm afraid.'

'How well did you know the Fitzpattens? What sort of couple were they?' Reg asked.

Those slanted eyebrows came together in a frown. 'I only knew them to pass the time of day with. I wasn't in their social league,

47

and didn't want to be. He was a cocky know-all of a sod, and he soon got bored with you if you weren't as sharp with your tongue and as clever as he was. He'd try and make you look stupid in front of other people, if he could. I couldn't stand the bloke, but women seemed to think he was the best thing since sliced bread. His wife is a beautiful woman. She's got everythings exactly in the right place, I can tell you, not too much nor too little, but she's still a stuck-up bitch. If you ain't rich or important she'll look down her nose at you as if you were something the cat's brought in. Anyway, they weren't here much of the time. She'd be off doing her modelling, and he travelled a lot, researching his books. It wasn't that often they'd be here together. A weird pair, if you ask me. They'd row a fair bit sometimes, you could hear them shouting at each other if their windows were open, but they always seemed to make up. Some people are like that, I suppose.'

'I gather he'd got a reputation as a womaniser, even if his wife was very attractive,' Reg suggested.

'That's what people do say. Women would chat him up just as often as he'd chat themup, but you don't know whether they'd then go off and do anything, do you? Not if you're not there to see them. I reckon a lot of it's just plain village gossip. I wouldn't pay too much attention to that, if I were you.'

'I've got to go and brief the CC, and I'll have to attend the damned autopsy before I can go and see Gwen. One of us has got to be there,' Walsh said reluctantly. As the senior investigating officer he really had to be there, but it was not a part of his job that he liked. He'd been to more post-mortems in his career than he could remember, but he was still not so hardened to the sight of a corpse being dismembered that the memory of it would not disturb his sleep for a few nights. The only job he hated more was that of tossing a live hand grenade into someone else's life by informing them of the sudden violent death of a close and beloved relative. He'd had to do that today with Mrs Fitzpatten, but fortunately the tears, the horror and the sheer helplessness of grief had been avoided in her case by the fact that she'd flaked out. That thought prompted a question.

'How is Mrs Fitzpatten, Brenda? Is she all right?'

'Sleeping like a log, Chief. The doctor gave her some pills, and we put her to bed. He said she was the second one he'd had to do that to today – apparently he attended the girl who found the body in the bunker this morning. Anyway, Mrs Fitzpatten will be out for the count for another eight or ten hours,' Brenda explained. 'We haven't been able to find a close friend or relative to come and be with her, though. It's all right for the moment, with the forensic people and us being here, but the doctor said we mustn't leave her on her own, because of the risk of her doing something stupid.'

Walsh nodded. 'I'll get the duty office to post a policewoman guard here for tonight. In the meantime there's the green-keeper to see, and the hotel night staff to interview, as well as the rest of the guests. You've got young Arthur Bryant and Alison Knott around somewhere, they can help, and when you've done that and the forensic team has finished, you can have a nose through all the papers that are lying about.' He pulled on his chin thoughtfully. 'With particular emphasis on any correspondence with women other than his wife. I'm sure you know what I mean. I have a feeling we might end up doing quite a lot of work on Fitzpatten's girlfriends.'

'I did hear something about it, down in the village, sergeant,' Grant Finlay, the head green-keeper acknowledged, nodding his head so vigorously that a few long strands of his fine white hair fluttered freely in the soft evening breeze. His face was lined, worn and weathered from the passing of time, but his body, though a little bent, was still youthfully lean and wiry. 'Young Fitzpatten's body was found buried in the big sand bunker at the eighteenth, they say.'

'That's right,' Reg Finch confirmed, bending down to fuss Finlay's long-eared spaniel, who had been taking inquisitive sniffs at his ankles. The dog submitted in cringingly meek politeness to the touch of the stranger's long fingers, but as soon as they were taken away, he scampered off to the more intriguing aromas to be found in the undergrowth among the trees that lined the fairway.

It was nearly dusk now, and although it still seemed fairly light out in the open, the distant trees and shrubs were beginning to fade into the gathering gloom.

'The Man Trap is what that bunker's called, sergeant. On account of our ghost.' Finlay's challenging tone begged for a sceptical response.

'Oh yes!' he went on seriously, having seen Reg's eyebrows dutifully rise disbelievingly. 'It could be important in your investigations, so I'd better tell you the story. It were a long time ago, of course. The Fitzpatten of the time, his daughter had got to the age when girls realise that boys aren't there just to play hide and seek with, so she started rolling her eyes at one of the Middlemarch boys, reckoning he'd learn her all the business about the birds and the bees. The Middlemarches are a family that lives out near Saffron Walden. The boy fancied her too, so it's said, so they planned to have an affair like what they'd read about in books, and the steamier the better. The only trouble was, in the normal run of things, they couldn't get enough time on their own together to get it started. Now Old Man Fitzpatten, he were no fool, and he had an idea that something was going on, and he didn't think much of it, because he didn't like them Middlemarches. Maybe they was Catholic, or didn't have enough money, I don't know; so he flatly forbids her to see the boy. Well, that's asking for trouble ain't it? Telling a woman what she can do or can't do. Anyway, as you'd expect, that sets her blood a-boiling and her heart a-beating something chronic, and it made her determined to defy her old man and have it off with that boy, come hell or high water. The trouble was it weren't long afore she couldn't think of nothing else but having it off, and it was driving her mad. So desperate like, 'cos she knew her old man weren't one to be trifled with, she sends her maid to the Middlemarch boy with a message telling him that if he didn't meet her that night in the old stone summerhouse and put her out of her misery, she'd go raving mad, or worse. The maid did what she was told, all right, but you know what women are like when they get hold of a right juicy bit of gossip like that. She blabbed it about, and Old Man Fitzpatten got to know. He was a wicked, evil old sod, he was. Do you know what he did? He had traps set. I've seen the like in museums. Bloody great bone-crunching man traps they were. He had them set on all the paths leading to that summerhouse, save the one from the main house, because the Middlemarch boy weren't likely to come in that way.

50

'It was a cold dark moonless night, that night was, with the wind a-whining and a-whistling through the trees like a thousand souls in torment. It were so black, you wouldn't have seen your fist, even if you had stuck it up in front of your nose. That young Middlemarch boy, he'd got the heat on him, just like the girl had, and he was a-coming whatever the weather, wild horses weren't going to keep him away. He knew he'd have the hide ripped off him if he were caught by Old Man Fitzpatten, so, cunning like, he leaves his horse back in the woods and creeps in on tiptoe, being dead careful. If he'd stayed that way, being dead careful, he might have been all right, but you know what his problem was? That Fitzpatten girl was a fair-looking piece, and I reckon he was thinking about him getting his hands on her boobs at last. Well, how can you think properly with thoughts like that in your head? So he got careless, and stuck his big foot smack bang into one of them bloody man traps. Snap crack, it would have gone, like a bloody land mine going off. It would damned near have cut his blooming leg off too, I reckon. There weren't no way he could get one of them things off him, not on his own, he couldn't, and he couldn't drag it along, 'cos it was chained to a great big tree. All he could do was yell, but it were the middle of the night and there weren't no one about to hear him, 'cos Old Man Fitzpatten had locked his daughter in her bedroom, and warned his men to stay indoors, hadn't he? That young Middlemarch boy must have been in agony. Have you ever seen a rabbit caught in a snare? The way it struggles to get free, and the more it struggles the tighter the wire gets round its leg, until the pain drives it mad and it dies. It must have been the same for that young boy. However much he screamed and shouted, there weren't no one going to come. When they found him next morning, he were as dead as a door post, stiff as a board. Shock, pain, or loss of blood, it don't make no difference which, once you're gone, does it? Well, there you are. Now his ghost wanders around on dark moonless nights, screaming his head off. I ain't seen him or heard him myself, but that's what they say he does, and that's why there's no love lost still between the Middlemarches and the Fitzpattens. They hate each others' guts, even now.'

Grant Finlay paused to give Reg Finch a sidelong look and a big grin. 'You don't believe me, do you? What you're saying to yourself is that a bit of pain on its own ain't enough to set a ghost a-haunting and a-howling, ain't you? I reckon you know a bit about ghosts, sergeant, and you're dead right. It needs something a lot worse than mere pain to make a spook go a-spooking. It needs something that screws up a man's vitals and drives hot irons deep in his soul where the agony will last for all eternity. Well, I'll tell you the rest of what happened, then you can make your own mind up. If this were a fairy story, which it ain't, the Fitzpatten girl should have died of a broken heart and be doing a bit of spooking of her own on dark moonless nights, but she didn't and she don't. Being locked in her room that night near drove her mad, and she was in a right old state when Fitzpatten let her out next morning. When he told her she would never have it off with that young Middlemarch lad, she flipped what was left of her lid. She said in her message that if she didn't have it off with that boy that night, she'd go raving mad, and that's what she did. She couldn't wait no longer. As soon as her old man was gone, she grabbed hold of the first feller she could get her hands on and she had the trousers off him in a twinkling, but that were the boot boy, and he were only a little lad. No doubt he did his best, but there weren't no way he could quench her raging fires, even if she was new to the game, so she had the footman next, then the butler, and that was only before breakfast. A quick snack and a cup of tea and she was off again. Now you know why the Middlemarch boy's ghost keeps on a-howling night after night? It weren't the man trap what did it. He keeps a-howling because he was the only man within miles who didn't get his leg across her that day. When you've wanted it as much as he had, and then your spirit sees the happy faces of them that's just had her, and a long queue of blokes lining up waiting their turn, that's just the kind of stuff what sends ghosts a-howling night after night. They do say she went to see the boy when he was all laid out proper in the church and would have given him his chance even then, if rigor mortis had set in, in the right place. Which was pretty decent of her, you must admit. Sex bloody mad them Fitzpattens are, the men and women alike, but then, the country folks around here are all a bit that way inclined too. Maybe it's the fresh air, or something in the water. There you are though, it wouldn't surprise me if it turned out that a Middlemarch had bashed young Fitzpatten's head in, though why he would want to go and bury him in my golf bunker, I don't know, and I'd only topped it up with sand the day before yesterday.'

'He wasn't bashed on the head,' Reg Finch said hastily, wanting to bring the conversation back to more sensible matters.

'Are you sure? Well, that's what they're saying in the village, and they usually knows what's going on,' Finlay replied in surprise.

'You'd recently topped up the bunker with sand. Why was that?'

'All the bunkers need topping up at least once or twice a year. It ain't like a links course on the coast, you know, where the wind blows sand in from the beach and dunes. Here the wind blows the bloody stuff away, especially when it's dry, and each time a player blasts his ball out, damn near a whole handful goes out as well.'

'Did you walk round the course last night? Did you see anything unusual?'

'Yes, I walked round here last night, same as I'm doing now, only you weren't with me, of course. That's when I work out what jobs need doing urgent like, and what order to do them in. It saves me time in the morning, see. No, I can't say I saw anything out of the ordinary. Nothing that would help you find a killer, anyway. If I were you I'd find out what all the Middlemarchs were up to last night. It might be one of them you're after.'

Finlay turned to stare at Finch's face with his cool grey eyes looking surprisingly youthful and mischievous. 'That's just one tip I'm giving you, and now I'll give you some more. If you want to find out a bit about young Gregory Fitzpatten's private life, you go and have a chat with young Lucy Stilito. She lives in the house with the red roses round the front door, right opposite the vicarage it is. Then when you've done that, go and have a chat with Houghton's missus, but don't you go a-telling anyone it was me as told you.'

5

'Would you like a cup of coffee, Reg?' Probationary Detective Constable Arthur Bryant asked as Finch came into the Fitzpattens' sitting-room after his interview with Finlay.

'I'd like one very much,' Reg replied, using the middle finger of his right hand to rub round his eyes as he looked round the room. The place had been tidied, and with the lights on to fight away the gathering dusk outside, the big room was mellow, warm and friendly.

'Alison can make you one,' Arthur declared, his boyish face creasing into a cheeky grin. 'She's much better at it than I am.'

'You are a lazy toad, Arthur. Would you like one too, Brenda?' Probationary Detective Constable Alison Knott got up from where she was sitting by a jumbled pile of papers and letters, on the floor near the leaded window. She was a cheerful, intelligent, stoutish young woman, who would have been none too pleased at the use of the word 'stoutish'. She went to great pains to control her calorie intake, and there really was no fat on her at all, or not very much – it was all muscle, which you'd expect with someone as big-boned as she was.

From the kitchen there soon came the faint sounds of drawers and cupboards being opened.

'Isn't Mrs Fitzpatten still asleep upstairs?' Reg asked, sitting down in one of the easy chairs.

'She's sound asleep,' replied Brenda. 'She came to a little while ago, and went to the bathroom, so I took her up a hot milky drink. She took another of the pills the doctor left for her, hopped back into bed, and was out again like a light, but she did say we were to make ourselves at home – so we are. Forensic have opened up that little locked room off the hallway, by the way. It was obviously a study, because there's a small desk and

54

a computer in there, but precious little else.' With that, Brenda set about reading more of the private correspondence of the Fitzpatten family.

Arthur Bryant, though, seemed unable to settle down to anything so mundane. He was intently studying the oak panels on the far wall. He ran his fingers down the lines of the linenfold carving, tried twisting the small Tudor rosettes set where the panel frames met, and occasionally tapped lightly on the wood with a knuckle.

'What on earth are you doing, Arthur?' Reg asked irritably. Bryant seemed to be messing about while others were working.

'Secret passages and priest-holes, Reg. This place is so old it must be riddled with them. I've found three panels that sound hollow, but I can't get any of them to move yet,' Arthur replied with barely disguised excitement in his voice.

'Lord, don't you start. I've just been hearing all about the ghost that goes a-howling and a-moaning on dark nights. The next thing you'll be telling me is that there's buried treasure here too,' Reg exclaimed scornfully.

'Well, and so there may be, Reg,' Brenda said with a laugh. 'Apparently one of the Fitzpatten family was a privateer in Good Queen Bess's golden days, and some of the loot was supposed to have been put away for a rainy day in a secret place that's now lost. I've just read a copy of the letter Fitzpatten wrote to someone who wanted to come and look for it with all the latest detection equipment. He was quite polite really. He said that his family records showed that a lot of money had been spent in that period on extending the house and acquiring more land, besides all that which had gone on profligate living, so that it was very unlikely that there was any of his ancestor's ill-gotten gains left by the time he'd died. So permission was refused.'

Arthur's mouth gaped open in wonder at that information. 'Even so, there might be some treasure left somewhere, and I bet I know where it might be – under that old summerhouse,' he declared.

'Nonsense, Arthur, you're way out,' Reg exclaimed. 'That was built in the early 1700s. It's obvious by the style.'

Arthur looked sulky. 'But there must be other hiding places or priest-holes,' he said tentatively.

Reg Finch shrugged, then smiled up at Alison Knott as she handed him his cup of coffee. He took a sip, but it was a bit too hot to drink straight away.

'There might have been hiding places for priests, Arthur, if the Fitzpattens were Catholic, but is it likely that Henry VIII would have had his row with the Pope, then sold one of the monasteries he was dissolving to a Catholic family? I doubt it. Anyway, if there ever were any hiding places for Jesuit priests here, the chances of them surviving all the rebuilding and modernisation that's gone on over the years are very remote.'

Arthur looked at Brenda, and saw that she was grinning at him broadly. When you got Reg talking on an historical topic, he would sometimes go on for quite a while.

'And if there were any priest-holes left, they wouldn't be easy to find. There were a couple of fellows, John Gerard and Nicholas Owen, who specialised in constructing hiding places in Catholic houses, but they made each new one as different from the others as they could, so that there would be no easy way to work out where they were. They weren't playing fun and games, Arthur, it was a desperately serious business, literally a matter of life or death. There was such a fear of Catholic plots to overthrow the Protestant monarchy, that if they found any holed-up Jesuit priest, he'd be tortured and killed without mercy. They had some very clever people working on both sides, so you won't find an entrance to a hiding place easily. They had them up chimneys and under hearths and stair treads and false beams. It's no good you tapping the panelling, Arthur, they're all fixed to battens, so naturally they'll sound hollow.'

Arthur Bryant stared ruefully at the panel beside him and reluctantly lowered the hand that was ready to continue the rapping process. 'What about secret passages and tunnels though, Reg? They'd have needed escape routes, wouldn't they?' he asked hopefully.

Reg smiled at him patiently. 'You've still got the same problem finding the entrance. Most of the passages discovered running from old houses turn out to be merely sewers and drains. Bucket loos at the bottom of the garden were a bit crude, even in those days. Elizabethan houses had lavatories, called garderobes. A shaft would go down the wall to a drain that would take the effluent well away from the house. No doubt they flushed it with buckets of water from time to time, when the smell got really bad. If you were in fear of your life you might be desperate enough to try wriggling down one, but it wouldn't have been easy. Obviously, if a house were being built on the site of an older property, a monastery for instance, the constructors would save themselves time and money by using the existing drainage system, and that could be quite sophisticated. There were some six hundred monks at Hasling Abbey, plus all the lay people, and that makes for a lot of sewage. They'd divert a stream with a good flow of water to drive their corn mill. Then they'd draw the water off down a covered, stone-lined culvert, and run it to the kitchens, bakery, brewery, and anywhere else that needed fresh water. After that the conduit would run to their reredorter, or lavatory, for washing, then it would pass under the toilets, to flush it all clean. Those culverts could be three, four, maybe five feet high. When anything like that is discovered by people digging ditches, the local newspapers usually make it out to be a secret passage built so that randy monks could meet up with randy nuns, but there's no historical evidence for that at all.'

'Have you finished your coffee, Reg? Right, Arthur,' Brenda interrupted firmly. 'It's time for us to go interviewing again. The night staff should be there now, but if there's any questions on your interview sheets about ghosts, treasure or secret passages, you might just find the Chief putting you on the fingertip search they'll be doing in the morning. Are you coming with us, Reg?'

Finch shook his head. 'Not at the moment. The green-keeper told me about a young woman in the village who can tell us all about Gregory Fitzpatten's private life. It may be merely village scandal, but he's a wise old bird, and there was something in the way he told me that makes me think I should take it seriously.'

'If you've got to go and see a young woman, Reg, I'd better go with you, to keep you out of trouble,' Alison Knott suggested hopefully. That sounded a more interesting job than mere routine interviewing.

'Yes, I think that might be wise. Did the boss send out a couple of uniformed policewomen to keep guard here, Brenda? Some more National Front members might pay another visit to finish whatever it was that they'd started. So we definitely mustn't leave this place unattended.'

57

The rose bushes that climbed round the front door of the house opposite the vicarage were, even in the gloom of twilight, a mass of colour. In fact, there were roses in full bloom everywhere in the little front garden. The occupier of this house was obviously more than just an enthusiast, for these were no ordinary happy-go-lucky roses left to fend for themselves most of the year. They were show quality, even prize quality.

'Yes, Lucy's here. It's to do with that Gregory Fitzpatten, is it?' Mrs Stilito asked, looking down at the warrant identification card Reg Finch was holding out for her to see. 'She was upset mortal bad when she got home. That awful Mrs Travers from the council estate told her. She was waiting for my Lucy to get off the bus, she was, with a big evil grin plastered all over her fat face. Oh, she's a nasty piece of work, she is. Lucy's been out in the back garden, on the seat underneath the old apple tree, ever since. If she ain't a-crying, she's a-staring into space looking so down in the dumps you'd reckon the world had come to an end. I can't do nothing with her and she ain't had her tea yet neither. One ain't supposed to speak ill of the dead, but I, for one, ain't going to lose any sleep now he's gone. Bloody trouble, he was.'

'Maybe so, Mrs Stilito, but if your Lucy is taking it bad then it might do her good to talk to complete strangers about things, to get it off her chest, if you understand me,' Reg Finch explained rather hesitantly. 'If she's in the garden, we'll go round the back. There's no need to show us. I'm sure we can find the way.' Some instinct told him that Lucy would talk more freely without her unsympathetic mother hovering about.

The apple tree was old, bent and knarled, long since pensioned off from the need to be pruned for bumper annual crops, and so it had been left to spread its twisted branches into a thick shady canopy of leaves. The girl sitting beneath it, on a rickety garden seat, was the complete antithesis of the tree. She was young, fresh and blooming, and she was a beauty. No slender fragile pastel flower of a girl, this one. Lucy Stilito was a ripe peach. When she turned to confront her visitors there was a grace and elegance to her movements that was as natural as day following night. Her dark shining hair framed a round, red-lipped face that had a complexion so clear and pure that it would drive a million

58

envious women to weep tears of frustration. A beautiful young woman, out of the top drawer, one might have said, until she opened her mouth and spoke. Her voice had the husky vibrant tones of a Marlene Dietrich but it also conveyed the impression that she was not one of the brightest of young people to come out of the state education system.

'How did you find out about me so quickly? Mrs Travers, was it?' Lucy asked hesitantly.

'That's not important. I just want you to tell me what you know about Gregory Fitzpatten, but firstly, a little about yourself. How old are you, Lucy, and where do you work?' Reg asked quietly. His voice seemed to convey to her a sense that he understood something of the grief she was suffering, and because of that perhaps she replied with less reluctance than she might otherwise have done.

'I'm seventeen, and I'm on a youth training scheme. I'm doing secretarial work at Palmers and Macintosh, the solicitors.'

'How long have you known Gregory Fitzpatten?' Alison Knott asked.

'I was only fourteen. Have I got to go through all this?'

'We need to know. Just tell us briefly,' Reg suggested.

'I met him in the woods, up by the golf course, when I was taking the dog for a walk. We talked a little, and then he put his arms round me and started kissing me and touching me. It got me feeling all soft and gooey inside, and, well, it just happened. I didn't know it were wrong, I didn't really understand what he was doing to me, but he were ever so gentle, he didn't hurt me at all, honest.'

'Was this just the once, or did it happen again?' Alison prompted.

'Oh! Over and over again after that. Just as often as he could get away from that stuck-up rotten old wife of his. She didn't understand him, see, that was why he needed me so badly. How could I say no? Besides, I'd gotten to like it by then, hadn't I? Well, I hadn't been having my periods proper all that long, and then all of a sudden they went and stopped. Mum made me go to the doctor's, and that's when the trouble all started. I was pregnant, wasn't I? Me dad hit the roof when Mum told him. He grabbed me in the kitchen and tried to lather me with that belt of his, like he used to do when I was a kid, but I weren't having none of that no more. I kneed him in the goolies and picked up a knife, and I told him. "As God's my witness," I said, "you just touch me with that there thing, and by Christ you'll get this stuffed right in your guts," I said. He backed off then, and went off shouting and screaming as how he was going to beat Gregory black and blue. He didn't, of course, because he ain't as big as him, but he come back saying as how Gregory said I was to have an abortion, and he'd pay, and that he'd sworn he'd never see me again.'

'So you had the abortion, and then went on seeing Gregory Fitzpatten in secret, did you? Without your father knowing?' Alison prompted.

Lucy nodded. 'Not straight away, though. After the abortion the doctor put me on the pill, so I haven't had that trouble again, have I? Me mum said there was plenty of other men about if all I wanted was a bloke grunting away on top of me, and so there is. I tried quite a few, honestly, but there weren't none as good at it as him. So I started meeting him again. Last week me dad found out. I think that Travers bitch told him. He asked me dead quiet like, was I having it off with Gregory again? I said, yes, I was, and that I was old enough to have it off with whoever I liked, without asking his permission. He didn't say nothing. He just looked at me icy like, and went off. That worried me, 'cos that ain't like him. He normally rants and raves about things.'

'I see. Now did Gregory ever talk to you about his work?' Reg asked.

'His books? Not a lot, but for the last month or two he's been getting ever so excited. He said the book he was writing now was really going to stir things up. Something to do with Hitler it was. I didn't understand quite what. It was going to make him famous, he reckoned, but he said he'd got to be real careful like, as they might be gunning for him.'

'Who might be gunning for him?' Alison asked with a frown.

Lucy shook her head and looked puzzled. 'Hitler, I suppose, or one of his mates. To be honest, I didn't really understand what it was about.'

'I've got one of the guests who says he actually saw Fitzpatten leave the hotel last night with someone, Brenda,' said the young

60

uniformed constable who was helping to take statements in the ground-floor room of the hotel usually reserved for conferences or meetings. 'Would you rather come and talk to him yourself?'

'That's what I'm here for,' Brenda Phipps replied cheerfully, getting up from where she'd sat near the door to keep a supervisory eye on proceedings. The paint-sprayed pale green trouser suit had been discarded in favour of one of the several spare outfits that she kept in the boot of her car for emergencies. The faded jeans and thick sweater, for use with rubber boots when tracking along hedgerows and across muddy fields, were hardly appropriate wear for someone supervising a team of interrogators in a posh hotel, and so her choice had to lie between a dark skirt and white blouse, or the colourful but rather gauzy Indian cotton party dress, which for some reason or other had fallen out of favour for private use. The skirt and blouse were much too like the hotel waitresses' uniforms, so the low-cut Indian cotton dress it had to be. It was certainly stylish, and a bit over the top for police work, but even the sarcastic Mrs Fitzpatten would have been hard put to find fault with it. There ought to have been a full-length slip to wear under it, but there wasn't one, so Brenda shrugged her shoulders and decided it didn't matter anyway. Under the mellow hotel lighting, the dress should not be too revealing.

That, apparently, was not the case, as she found out when she approached the podgy-faced, beak-nosed male hotel guest with the close-waved grey hair.

'Wow!' he declared, rising hurriedly to his feet and gazing in undisguised admiration at the vision in wispy Indian cotton who had just introduced herself to him as Detective Constable Phipps, of the Cambridgeshire Constabulary's Criminal Investigation Department. Momentarily bereft of coherent speech he may have been, but there was nothing wrong with the working of his eyes.

'Well, I never,' he said eventually. 'My opinion of the British police force has risen dramatically during the last few seconds. I can assure you, young lady, that I will admit to any charge you might bring against me, provided it's you who beds me down for the night in a cell. You give all the appearance of being an angel, but I hope you're not, I hope you're depraved and wicked.'

Brenda responded with a blandly cold look that was intended to convey the message that such excesses of gallantry were, in her opinion, quite sickening. She sat down on the chair by the interview table and picked up the partly completed statement form.

'Well, Mr Pitt. I understand you saw the dead man last night,' she said hastily, trying to prevent an embarrassed flush coming to her face.

'Very nearly right,' Pitt replied with a broad grin, evidently well pleased with the fact that he'd clearly disconcerted her, 'but he wasn't a dead man at the time, unless it was his ghost I saw walking about.'

'You say you were in the hotel lounge at shortly after nine o'clock yesterday evening,' Brenda said, having quickly read what was already written on the statement form. 'What happened then?'

'Well, the man, of whom that is a photograph,' he pointed to the glossy print on the table, 'or his ghost, came out of either the bar or the dining-room, I didn't notice which. Anyway, he was heading towards the main door when a fellow came up to him. "I want a word with you," he said. It was the tone of his voice which really caught my attention, because it was aggressive. Well, the dead man obviously knew him, because he said, "Oh Lord, not you again. Not in here – outside." Then they both went out of the door and walked off together. Is that of any help to you?'

'It could be. What was the fellow like? Can you describe him?' Brenda asked.

'Shortish, mousy-haired, and scruffy. He might have been a gardener, or a tractor driver – certainly not a hotel guest. Now look, I've obviously been very helpful, so I think you should show your gratitude by having a drink with me.'

For some men the chatting up of a lone woman in a hotel is a sport of fantasy designed to inflate their manly egos while away from their wives, safe in the knowledge that their extravagant propositions will almost certainly be rejected. If the woman appeared to be taking them seriously, however, it could result in a severe shock to the system, and not a little fear of the possible consequences. This fantasising male was definitely disconcerted when Brenda gave him a radiant smile and said, 'Yes, I'll take

62

you up on that. You can buy me a coffee in the foyer while we ask the hotel reception staff if they can put a name to your description of this mousy-haired man. I'll meet you there in five minutes.'

It had just occurred to her that those pale green trousers had only just the odd spot of paint on them. Those, worn with the white blouse, would prevent her feeling that she was being auditioned for a full frontal naked sex scene in some pornographic video.

The hotel foyer had once been a magnificent room. It still was, of course, but there was no denying that its present use as a hotel reception area had destroyed much of the atmosphere it once must have had. It was wide and long, with a high plastered ceiling on which had been painted a vast park-like landscape scene of sunlit rolling hills and shady leafy copses, in which a number of near-naked ladies gazed at a small group of grossly overweight male children with wings, who were unwisely being allowed to gambol around shooting lethal-looking arrows. The walls were panelled with plain light oak, and there was a huge carved stone fireplace at one end, before which had been set a large display of dried flowers. A broad sweeping staircase, with a much-polished handrail supported by a profusion of barley-corn twisted posts, led to the upper floors.

Robin Sainsbury, the professional golfer, stirred uneasily in his chair in a corner of the foyer. He'd sat himself there so that he could watch the stairs, and yet be as far away from the main door and the reception desk as possible. He wanted to be inconspicuous, but it was a busy place. A veritable crossroads from the main door to the stairs, as well as from bar to dining-room, and it was amazing how often those people passing through seemed to catch his eye, and stare back at him with indifferent superiority, as though he might be some ragged Bombay beggar displaying his twisted crippled limbs on a dusty pavement. Some of them, those who had been watching the golf tournament that morning, might just recognise him as one of the players, but they wouldn't be the slightest bit interested in why he was sitting where he was, with a long since drained cup of coffee on the low table beside him, and a long since read glossy magazine still lying open on his knees.

Why was he wasting his time sitting there? Why had he been sitting there for nearly two and a half hours? His mind had given up asking himself those questions, because his mind wanted logical answers, and there was no logic in what he was doing. He was in the grip of irrational feelings, and paramount was the desire to be with his golf partner of the morning – Amanda Knightly. While she had been so distressed he had cradled her in his arms and felt the softness and warmth of her. She had clung to him too, and had needed him. Now he couldn't get her out of his mind.

Logic told him that the events by the bunker had been an emergency situation for her, and that she would have behaved like that with anyone. What he had done did not create a special relationship between himself and Amanda Knightly, and any attempt to assume that it did would result in a chilling rebuff. Logic told him that he was being emotionally unstable, and showing it. The death of his wife had left him in shock and repressed his physical needs, but now those floodgates had cracked, and there was a whole torrent of emotions ready to flow out; like a new-born chick who latches on to the first thing it sees as its mother, so Robin Sainsbury had latched on emotionally to Amanda Knightly.

Her room was upstairs, and she might come down. That was why he was waiting, but he could not stay there for ever. He made a half-hearted attempt to get up and go, but sank back again, and turned a page of the magazine. When he again looked up at the stairs, on them, coming down, was Amanda Knightly – a pale frail-looking slip of a girl in brown slacks and a white blouse, with the strap of a bag over one shoulder, and a white woolly cardigan in the hand that was not clutching the banister rail.

Robin Sainsbury's heart started to pound as he stood up, prepared, it seemed, to advance and take on the chin whatever rebuffs fate had in store for him.

The woman's face bore an anxiously thoughtful expression as she looked down, carefully watching her feet move safely on to each of the steps below. Perhaps the movement Robin made as he got to his feet caught her eye, for she suddenly looked in his direction, and then without any change of expression, her head turned away.

Some sense seeped back into Robin's brain. Clearly she had recognised him, but equally clearly, she now had no need of him.

The best thing he could do was get the hell out of there, back into his own safe sterile world, and forget the whole thing. He set off towards the door. If she turned to look at him again he would smile politely, ask her how she was, and be on his way.

Suddenly she was not only looking at him, but taking a step forward to intercept him. Her face was very pale and her grey eyes seemed enormous.

'Robin!' she said thickly, the effort of talking making her swallow several times. 'I'm so glad to see you. I'm dreadfully sorry about this morning. You must think me such fool. I'm so sorry. Thank you for being so understanding.'

'There's no need to thank me,' Robin heard his own voice utter. 'It was enough to frighten anyone out of their wits. Anyway, how are you now? You still look very pale.'

Amanda shivered and her bottom lip trembled. 'I'm all right, as long as I don't think about that hand coming up out of the sand. It'll give me nightmares for the rest of my life, I know it will. It seems as if it was reaching up and saying, "Here you are, here's your ball." Isn't that nonsense?' There was a tinge of hysteria in her nervous laugh.

'You mustn't think about it. Wouldn't it be better if you went back to bed and took some more tranquillisers?' Robin suggested hastily. 'You'll probably feel better in the morning.'

Amanda shook her head determinedly. 'I took a couple of them about an hour ago, but they didn't work. I've been lying there on my bed thinking myself silly. I don't want to be on my own any more just now – besides, I feel hungry, and a bit of food inside me might stop me feeling so sick, but I don't fancy eating in there.' She inclined her head towards the dining-room. 'The people I work with will only make a fuss, and I couldn't stand that.'

'That's no problem. I can drive you into Cambridge for a meal, if you like. I haven't eaten either. It's not far, and the fresh air might do you good,' Robin suggested eagerly. It was as though all those mental qualms he'd had while he'd been waiting had never been, for Amanda was nodding. Now he could relax, be himself, and enjoy her company.

Finding a candle-lit table for two in a Cambridge Trinity Street restaurant was no problem that evening.

'Who was the man, anyway? The man in the bunker, I mean,' Amanda asked, putting down the now half-empty second glass from the bottle of white wine she'd chosen to have with her lasagne. This Robin Sainsbury had a pleasant, friendly, safe sort of face, and rather nice eyes, she thought.

Robin shrugged his shoulders. 'A chap who lived in the old wing of the hotel. His family used to own the place originally, I understand.'

'But what was he doing in the bunker?'

'Not a lot,' Robin replied light-heartedly. 'I really don't know.'

Amanda's grey eyes looked directly at him in a strange sort of way, and he couldn't read the expression in them. Her face wasn't exactly a poker face, it was too pretty for that; maybe it was more of a business face, a negotiating face, trained to give nothing away until an advantageous deal had been struck. Maybe she was just summing him up. So he smiled back reassuringly.

'Are you married, Robin?' she asked shyly, looking down at her plate.

'Not now. My wife died two years ago. I'm not sure if I've got over it yet,' he replied bluntly.

Amanda looked up in surprise, then reached out in sympathy to touch his hand. Her fingers were soft and cool, and that gentle contact sent an electric tingle running up the flesh of his arm.

'That must have been awful. Me, I'm just a common divorcee. He left me and went off to do some wheeling and dealing in Hong Kong. It rather shook me at the time, so I put my head down and worked hard to take my mind off things. I haven't met anyone who I . . . well . . . never mind.'

She leaned forward to turn Robin's hand over and study his palm. 'You've a strong lifeline, Robin, and these mean you will succeed in what you're doing,' she went on, pointing to some tiny creases. 'You've got nice hands, real man's hands, gentle but strong. Just the sort a good golfer should have. You're a very fine player. I saw that this morning. Did you ever play in any of the majors?'

Robin smiled and shook his head ruefully. 'Like every player my dream was to win the Open. I did try to get on the circuit, but each time I played a qualifying round my game just fell apart. Perhaps I haven't got the nerve for the really competitive game. I'd like to have another go one day though, before I get too old.'

Her face grinned up at him in the flickering candle-light. 'You should. Maybe that's the success shown in your lifeline. Fancy, you striding down the eighteenth at St Andrews with me as your caddie, tied for the lead with the PGA and Masters' champion who is also the world's number one. The crowd are on their feet, cheering and shouting because your ball is on the green and the American's is in the bunker. He plays a brilliant shot out of the sand, that sets everyone gasping in amazement, and gets to within a foot of the hole. Now you've got a twenty-footer across the worst humps and hollows you've ever seen on a green, to win the Open by one stroke. The crowd goes deadly silent as you and I crouch down to work out the line. No one's holed from there all week and you'll be lucky to get down in three, let alone two.' Her eyes were very bright and a little hazy. 'You strike the ball firmly and boldly. It snakes up and round the hollows, and it seems as though it'll miss by a yard, but then it curves in sharply. Will it bend in enough? The gallery groans as the ball teeters on the edge, but then it drops in and the crowd goes absolutely wild. England's hero, Robin Sainsbury, beats the best in the world and is Open champion. Hurrah!'

Robin laughed. 'Wouldn't that be wonderful? Would you really caddie for me if I played in the Open?'

'You bet. I wouldn't miss it for the world. I'd have my hair done and my face lifted, and wear the sexiest outfit I could find, to put all the other fellows off their strokes.'

'You'd do that all right, but you won't need your face lifting. It's lovely enough as it is.'

Amanda's smile was even mistier now, and her soft hand came to touch his again. This time the tingles ran up his spine, bounced about in his head, rang a few bells, then ran all the way down again.

'That's a nice thing to say, Robin. You make me feel . . . well, like a real woman again.'

'You're a real woman, all right, Amanda. Maybe one day, if I can afford it, I'll have a go and try qualifying for the Open,' Robin said quietly. He was getting a little concerned at the amount of wine she was drinking. Alcohol, sleeping tablets and tranquillisers did not go well together. He'd only had one glass himself, because he was driving, but now the bottle was nearly empty.

'There's a good prize for the professional who wins the tournament tomorrow. That would help,' Amanda pointed out.

'Well, we're three strokes in the lead, but do you think you could play another seventeen holes, after what you've been through?' Robin asked. That money would certainly come in useful, if he could get it.

Amanda's face took on an expression of anguish, as though the thought of playing golf the next day did not appeal to her. 'I don't honestly know. I don't think I could ever play another bunker shot.'

'Well, that's that then. We'll have to withdraw. Never mind.'

'No, it's not "that then",' she said with a determined frown. 'I've got to get over it. It's like falling off a horse, not that I've ever done that, because I don't like horses, but you've got to get up and back on again, or else you'll lose your nerve, they say. That's what I should do. I ought to play that course again, and when the police have finished with that bunker, I ought to play out of it over and over again, until it doesn't bother me. Robin, I've made up my mind. I'm not going to check out of the hotel tomorrow when the tournament's over. I'm going to take a few days' holiday, and stay here until that bunker doesn't give me nightmares. Would you help me exorcise my ghost, Robin? Somehow I don't think it would quite work without you there.' She looked at him anxiously and rather sleepily; and a little muscle near her left eye started to flutter nervously.

Robin nodded seriously. However much she might try to appear relaxed, she was clearly still very tense inside. It was understandable. 'Sleep on it. There's plenty of time to decide what's best, in the morning,' he suggested wisely. 'Now I'm going to take you back to the hotel. You look all in.'

She was certainly not quite with it later, when he helped her out of his car at the hotel car-park; she was visibly rocking on her feet.

'Whoops,' she said in surprise, clutching tightly at his arm. 'Is it me going round, or is it the world? I daren't go through reception like this. Someone is bound to see me, and they'll say I'm drunk, but I'm not, really I'm not,' she insisted. 'Help me up the back stairs. That door over there.'

By clinging tightly to Robin's arm and walking slowly, she made it to the long corridor on the first floor without mishap.

After fumbling in her bag for the key, she opened the door and together they lurched in. He helped her over to the single bed where she could sit down.

Then there was an awkward stony silence.

Each looked at the other in shocked amazement and almost horror at suddenly finding themselves in a place where only the intimate should be together – a bedroom. After a few moments Robin moved towards the door.

'I'd better be going. I'll call in and see you in the morning,' he said quietly. Then to his surprise her face crumpled like a hurt child's, and she burst into tears.

'I'm frightened,' she sobbed helplessly. 'I know I'm being silly, but as soon as I close my eyes I'm going to see that damned man's hand holding my ball in the bunker. I'm scared to be alone.'

Robin went to sit on the bed beside her and put his arm round her shoulders consolingly. 'Take it easy, love. Take it easy. There's nothing to be afraid of. You get into bed, and, if you like, I'll stick around until you're fast asleep.'

Her big grey weeping eyes looked up at him, and then she shook her head vigorously. 'Then when I wake up I'll be alone in the dark. I'll go screaming mad. I know I will.' Her voice was rising shrilly in desperation.

'Steady on. Steady on,' Robin said hastily. 'Do you want me to stay? I can sleep in that armchair over there. It looks reasonably comfortable.'

'Yes. I'm sorry, but yes, I do want you to stay. But bring the chair over by the bed, where I can reach out and touch you, so I'll know you're there, if I wake up,' she insisted.

'All right. All right. Have it your own way. You just get ready for bed.'

He turned politely away while she undressed and got between the sheets. He switched off the light and settled himself in the armchair by the bed, prepared for an uneasy vigil. That was to be made more uncomfortable for him, because Amanda was making sure he couldn't leave her alone in the dark; she'd taken one of his hands and was holding it on her pillow, and now her cheek lay on his outstretched fingers. Almost immediately she was asleep, leaving Robin to reflect on a most extraordinary day.

That its events should have brought him here, to the bedroom of an almost unknown naked girl, was almost beyond belief. Inevitably fantasies stirred in his lonely mind. Given these circumstances, surely other men would have taken advantage of Amanda's semi-comatose helpless state, and already have had sex with her. In fact, she had been so frightened that if he'd demanded sex as the price of his staying, he felt sure she would have agreed. He felt ashamed at his failure to act like other men, for his desires were stirring strongly within him, but on reflection he felt glad that he hadn't. If a relationship was going to develop between them, it would be better if it did so in a natural way.

Later on he wasn't quite so sure that was the right thing. Amanda's slight movements caused the sheets to slip off her shoulders, and since his eyes had become used to the curtained darkness, he could see part of her nakedness quite well. The urges that sight aroused made the prospect of him dozing off much more unlikely. Still, nature works in funny ways, and eventually he slept.

It was later when a light pulling on his arm woke him.

Amanda lay on her back, with her head turned towards him, staring open-mouthed at him with wide puzzled eyes. The palm of his hand was now held firmly against her breast.

It was not logic but unconscious instinct that made him bend his head forward to kiss her lips and reach out in growing desire for her responsive body.

Nature may work in funny ways, but sometimes it is pretty predictable.

'How are you feeling now, love?' Sidney Walsh asked his wife. There was tenderness in his voice, an affectionate smile on his lips, and worry in his eyes.

'I'm fine,' Gwen replied in a tired listless voice. 'Are you looking after yourself properly, Sidney? Don't forget those little shepherd's pies I've made for you. They're in the second drawer of the freezer. All you've got to do is defrost them and give them three minutes in the microwave.'

Walsh nodded. 'I'll have one when I get home, but are you feeling better now than you were this morning?' If she was, he really didn't think she looked it. There was perhaps a little more

70

colour to the skin of her face now, it was a shade pinker than the pillows, but in truth it didn't look that much healthier than the waxy dead white skin of the now well-dissected body of Gregory Fitzpatten. The pathologist was having a coffee break, so Walsh had hurried from the mortuary to the main hospital building and to Gwen's bedside.

It was difficult to switch from the professionally cold and dispassionate attitude he'd had towards the body on the slab in the mortuary, to one of genuine concern for the woman he loved, who was lying in the hospital bed.

Even as they recounted irrelevant anecdotes of the day's events, the pathologist's comments were re-running themselves compulsively like a videotape in his mind. The meticulous examination of Fitzpatten's body had revealed no wounds other than the one to his head, and so the dissecting had been mainly to remove those organs in which traces of toxins or poison might possibly be found. However, the expert opinion was that the cause of death was entirely due to the gun shot. The pathologist's searching in the skull cavity had been particularly gruesome. It appeared that the small bullet, now much distorted but of a calibre of approximately .22, had been fired from a close range. It had passed through the brain, and splintered and shattered the cheekbone on the other side. Those splinters had torn through the hair and outer skin, but the bullet itself had not had the power or velocity to force an exit; it had ricocheted around inside the skull cavity, coming to rest not far from the point of entry. That much he'd already deduced from observation, he thought to himself, even as he related to Gwen the story of the ruin of Brenda Phipps's light green trouser suit, with some humorous additions. The pathologist had declared that the lack of a weapon meant that the man's death should be treated as murder, but the most important thing about the autopsy was that now the man's clothing was available for detailed forensic examination. The marks, stains and microscopic debris which had been caught in the fibres of that material, when identified, could, should or might tell enough of a story to enable him to be certain just where the man had been killed, and how he had been transported to the bunker at the eighteenth green. Hopefully too, he might learn who had pulled the trigger that had fired the handgun.

71

There was much to think and worry about when Walsh arrived back at his lonely home. The defrosting of a shepherd's pie was something he did not even consider. A round of bread and marmalade and a bowl of cornflakes sufficed to dull any pangs of hunger, and when the washing machine had been duly stuffed with dirty clothes he took a sleeping pill and went to bed. There he prayed himself to sleep with requests that Gwen's biopsy report would be favourable, and that she would look a lot better tomorrow than she had done today.

6

The next morning dawned as bright as the previous day. The sun, the blue sky, and the freshness of the air would engender in many people the desire to get out and about, to enjoy a day that promised to be one on which it was good to be alive.

Such thoughts no doubt passed through the minds of Brenda Phipps and Reg Finch when, at a time most folks had yet to decide whether to have an egg or cornflakes for breakfast, they made their way into the Hasling Abbey Hotel's small conference room. Sidney Walsh was already there.

'First things first,' he said. 'The pathologist's estimate of the time of Fitzpatten's death is pretty vague, because of the insulating effects of the sand, and because there is no way of telling how long the body had been buried in it. Between eight and ten the previous night, is the best we're going to get. Anyway, this is now officially a full-scale murder enquiry, so we'll need to formalise yesterday's activities with written reports, in the usual way. So let's now compare notes, then we can work out how best to proceed. Reg, how did you get on?'

'I talked to Myres, the professional at the golf shop. He hadn't seen anything suspicious on the night Fitzpatten died, but he did confirm what Houghton had told us, that the dead man was a womaniser. I didn't get any names though. Then I saw Finlay, the green-keeper. He's no fool, even if he did tell me a long tall story about why the bunker where the body was found is called the Man Trap. There's supposed to be a deadly feud between the Fitzpattens and a family called Middlemarch,' Reg explained.

'That's interesting. One of the hotel staff, one of the chambermaids or waitresses, is a Middlemarch,' Brenda interrupted, having scanned down a list of names.

73

'I'm not surprised,' Reg went on. 'Anyway, Finlay came over to me as a pretty shrewd fellow, and he gave me some tips on Fitzpatten's affairs. One we'd guessed already, that's the hotel manager's wife, the other was a young girl called Lucy Stilito, who lives in the village.'

'Stilito?' Brenda exclaimed in surprise. 'I'm sorry. I didn't mean to interrupt. Go on, Reg.'

'I took Alison with me, and went to see her. She's a real rosy-cheeked milkmaid type, who's none too bright. A bit like the girl in *Oklahoma* who can't say no. Fitzpatten seduced her when she was only fourteen and got her pregnant. Her dad got him to pay for an abortion, which he did, and also to promise to leave her alone, which he didn't. Now here comes the interesting bit. This Lucy said that Fitzpatten told her that the book he was currently writing was about Hitler, and that it was going to make him really famous because it was going to upset a lot of people, but he was having to be very careful, since those people might be gunning for him. Now how true that is, I don't know, because Fitzpatten was obviously spinning her all sorts of lines, but it might possibly tie in with the raid by those National Front thugs yesterday. Hitler is one of their idols, isn't he?'

'Headquarters should sort out the identities of those two today, if they've got criminal records, but if Fitzpatten was writing a book, then the manuscript ought to be in the Tudor wing somewhere,' Walsh suggested.

'I didn't see any signs of a book manuscript. It's certainly not in the papers from the wrecked bureau, Chief,' Brenda said. 'But I've got something to add to Reg and his Stilito business, and it'll tighten up on the time of death. One of the hotel guests saw Fitzpatten going out of the foyer at just after nine on the night he died, but before he got to the door he was accosted by a shortish, mousy-haired scruffy-looking man. The reception staff say that describes a local man from the village – by name, Stilito. He must be the girl's father. Fitzpatten didn't seem too pleased to see him. "Oh Lord, not you again," he said. Anyway, they went out of the hotel together.'

Walsh looked pleased. 'Well done. That's what I like to hear. An aggressive meeting close to the time of death. Maybe this is going to be one of our easiest murders to solve. Was there anything else of interest from the interviews of the other guests and hotel staff?'

Brenda shook her head. 'I'm afraid not.'

'Right. Let's have a plan of action for this morning. There's Mrs Fitzpatten to interview, if she's recovered from her shock sufficiently. You and I ought to do that, Brenda. Then there's this Stilito fellow. You see him, Reg. Take Alison or Arthur with you. Perhaps you can also manage the Middlemarch woman and Mrs Houghton as well. Hopefully this afternoon Richard Packstone will give us an initial briefing on what the forensic team are getting up to. We'll compare notes again then, I think. We might have a better idea of where we are going.'

'Yes, inspector, I am all right now, thank you,' Mrs Lynda Fitzpatten said in her soft well-modulated voice.

Walsh stared at the beautiful face. There were some signs of stress, but other facial signs that he would have expected to see were missing. A newly made widow ought still to show shock, grief and despair only twenty-four hours after learning of her sudden loss, but it would appear that Mrs Lynda Fitzpatten was made of sterner stuff than others of her sex. Clearly she was not prepared for her way of life to be affected by any incident, serious or otherwise. She had given great pains to her make-up. Her carefully tidied brows had been subtly darkened to emphasise the brilliance of her eyes. Her lips were more exquisitely shaped than ever nature could have achieved unaided, and each hair on her head seemed to have been individually put into its allotted place. Today she wore a simple lacy beige sleeveless top and brown slacks, and made them seem elegant. She was a very beautiful woman. If she had been the siren calling to Homer's Odysseus, his ship would definitely have gone headlong on to the rocks. If this woman set out to lure a man, she would have few failures.

'You put a guard on me last night, while I was lying weak and helpless, inspector. That was very kind of you,' the vision acknowledged, awarding him the titbit of a smile in gratitude.

'It seemed a wise thing to do,' Walsh said calmly. 'You are a photographers' model, I understand?'

'Didn't you know that? Did you really need to ask?' Lynda Fitzpatten's immaculate eyebrows rose up in a questioning frown. 'You must have seen my face in magazines and advertisements a hundred times over. I'm the model for DeMarchant, you can't have missed the TV advert, and I've been on the cover of *Vogue* a million times.'

'Is that indeed so?' Walsh muttered awkwardly. Out of the corner of his eye he could see Brenda Phipps almost traumatised with soundless laughter. He frowned, and went doggedly on. 'I must read the wrong papers. I'm afraid some of my questions may seem rather pointless to you, but I need to ask them, all the same. Now, I understand that you use the surname DeMilne for professional purposes, that you've been married to Gregory Fitzpatten for two years, and besides this Tudor wing here, you have a flat in London and an apartment in Rome. Is that correct?'

'Nearly. This place is Gregory's. I own the other two, although you wouldn't think so, the way he treats them. He's spent more time in London and Rome this past twelve months than he has here, in this spooky old place.'

'Spooky?'

'Too right. It looks nice, and it's got real style, but living in it takes some getting used to, I can tell you. All the creaky groaning noises, and the feeling that Gregory's dirty-minded old ancestors are ogling at me when I'm undressing. It's worse when I'm on my own. Gregory said that the noises were all the old timbers expanding and contracting when they get warm or cool down, and maybe he was right, but it still sounds to me like people moving about who aren't really there. Anyway, spooks or no spooks, I won't be sleeping here tonight, I shall stay in the hotel. I've packed all I want in some suitcases. They're in the bedroom. Since you seem to have taken over the house, inspector, perhaps you'll be kind enough to see that they're taken round for me. I don't know when you want Gregory's funeral to be, but I must tell you now that in three days' time I am going to Antigua. I've got to have my picture taken on the beach wearing a wet skimpy cotton shirt, while I eat a chocolate bar or something, and pretend I'm having an orgasmic thrill.'

'Would you mind telling me where you were the day before yesterday, and where you spent the night before last?' Walsh asked, blotting out any mental pictures of this woman wearing nothing but a skimpy wet cotton shirt.

'The morning before yesterday I was in the London flat until about eleven, that was when the decorators arrived, then I spent two hours being photo'd in a very low-cut blouse just to show my boobs while I bent over the keyboard of a new personal computer. After lunch it was diamonds, real diamonds and long velvet dresses in Bond Street. I enjoyed doing that. Then it was up to Nottingham, for an early morning session yesterday at the castle for a fashion feature for *Elle*. I mean early too, before the locals were about. I do work hard, as you can see.'

'How did you travel from London to Nottingham? By car?'

Lynda Fitzpatten shook her head slowly, presumably so as not to disturb any of those carefully positioned hairs. 'No, by train. I do not have a car.'

'But you can drive?'

'Yes, but I don't choose to. I prefer to travel by train, plane or taxi. It's so much nicer letting someone else have all the hassle.'

'Perhaps you'd be kind enough to jot down the details of your journey to Nottingham. Times, hotel and who you were with. Just for the record. Now, I want to talk to you about the book your husband was writing. First of all, do you know where he kept the manuscript, and his notes?'

'They'll be in his study, if they're anywhere.'

'His study being the room with the low door, off the hall?'

'That's right. His own personal private den, where no one else was welcome.'

'We haven't been able to find them in there.'

The shrug of her slim shoulders indicated an almost complete lack of interest in the subject.

'But you know about the book? It does exist?' Walsh asked with a deepening frown.

'Oh yes, it's about somewhere. I don't know why on earth you're interested though, it was only about the life of some old hermit priest.'

'A what?' Walsh exclaimed in surprise.

'Yes, an old hermit priest who lived in Germany in the 1930s, who Gregory said he thought ought to be made a saint. Well, that was the story he told when he dragged me with him all round Rome and half of Italy, to the places where he had traced other members of the old priest's order. Hieronymites, they all were, or something like that. I'd thought hermits lived in caves, but this lot didn't. Anyway, they were all long since dead and buried. I had to provide the charm while he chatted up people to get permission to grub through dirty old boxes full of dusty papers. Not my cup of tea, I can assure you. Mind you, I didn't believe a word of what he was telling them. I do not believe that Gregory would be wasting his time on some poxy old hermit, not unless there was a chance of getting a best-selling book out of it. That was what Gregory was after. A best-seller, that would make him famous.'

Walsh was frowning hard, and looking rather puzzled. 'Are there any hiding places here that you know of, where he might have kept his papers?' he asked.

Lynda Fitzpatten gave a titter. 'You're like everyone else. Just because this place is old you think it's full of secret passages, ghosts and buried treasure. Enid Blyton has a lot to answer for.'

'Did your husband have any enemies? Anyone who might have held a grudge against him?' Walsh asked.

Mrs Fitzpatten gave a giggle this time. 'There must be dozens. Gregory was fourteen, so he told me, when his school matron took him in hand, so to speak, and stole his virginity. He's been cuckolding husbands and deflowering innocent and not so innocent maidens ever since. God knows how many kids he's fathered, because he was never one for taking precautions.'

'All right. What about recent visitors?'

Lynda Fitzpatten thought for a moment. 'I was away so often I didn't get to know much about what he was doing, but I do know that a few days ago a Catholic priest was going to come and see him. It stuck in my mind because when Gregory told me, he also said that he might as well face up to the storm now as later, and I thought that sounded a bit strange. It was a Father Monserrat, or some name like that. Now, I have a lot to do this morning. My taxi will be here in ten minutes, and I need to tidy up a bit first, so you'll have to excuse me now. I'm having lunch in Cambridge with Myra Burton, you know. She'll cheer me up. She was a top model in her day, but she's well past it now, poor old thing. All she's fit for are corset ads and dresses for the fuller figure.' She stopped talking, and for a moment looked a trifle sad. 'Gregory's dead now, and I'm very very sorry about it, really I am, even if he was a bastard to me at times, but I am not going to let him spoil my life, so there. I'm sure he wouldn't want me to do that. Now I must fly. Don't worry, I'll jot down the details of my alibi for the other night before I go. Then you

78

can play around here looking for your hidy-holes to your heart's content. Lock the place up when you've finished and give the key to the hotel manager.' Then she got to her feet, and flitted gracefully away.

Brenda Phipps's eyes were moist with laughter. 'She gave you a hard time, Chief. You should have left her for me to sort out. All those soft airs and languid graces are her stock in trade, honed to perfection, but underneath all that she's a cold and calculating money-making machine, who can fight tooth and claw, if she needs to.'

Walsh felt irritated, but Brenda was right, he had never been in full control of that interview, and now that she'd gone he remembered another question he should have asked – about whether her husband had made a will. That would have to wait, there was no point in crying over spilt milk.

'Well you can check out her alibi then, but I don't understand where this hermit monk she talked about comes in, Brenda. There were some letters in the bureau from his agent or publisher, weren't there? Maybe they've got the manuscript. Give them a ring, will you, Brenda? But are you absolutely certain there was nothing stored on that computer's hard disc?' Walsh asked.

Brenda frowned. 'That wasn't what I said. The software programs are all there, but there's no stored input data at all. Obviously when Fitzpatten finished using it he transferred his work to floppy discs, and he must have put those somewhere else because the only ones I could find were his back-up program discs.'

'We'd better have another look round then, just in case we've missed something obvious. If we still don't find what we're after, this afternoon we'll get Reg, Arthur and Alison here, and assume there's a secret hidy-hole somewhere. Maybe the famous five of us can crack the riddle of the missing manuscript, even if we don't have a dog with us. I used to like Enid Blyton's books when I was a kid, and I'm hanged if I'm too old now to enjoy a spot of priest-hole hunting.'

John Frederick Stilito was an employee of the garden centre situated near the main road, a mile or so on the far side of the village from the hotel.

'Yes, it's true. I did go and see Fitzpatten that evening. I can't deny it and I won't deny it,' he exclaimed aggressively, bending down to pick up and replace the price board of the nearby garden seat that had been used as a Frisbee by a precocious four-year-old who was obviously intent on training himself to become the country's biggest yob and was leaving a wide trail of destruction behind him as he followed his oblivious parents through the store.

'Are you sure you wouldn't prefer to go somewhere more private than this?' Reg Finch asked.

'I can't leave the store while the boss is out, but it'll be quieter over by the greenhouses.' This reply from John Stilito was much less spirited than his first. He had tried to adopt an assertive stance for this interview, but even after such a short time he had been unable to maintain it. There was a tired helpless look in his dark brown eyes and the evidence of much stress on the florid skin of his face.

'Did you drive up to the Abbey Hotel that evening, or did you walk?' Reg wanted to know.

'I was in the Land Rover, doing some deliveries. We does that, you see. Heavy stuff or big stuff, what people can't get in their car boots, if they pays a bit extra we takes it round for them, provided it ain't too far. That Fitzpatten weren't at home, but I knew the bastard sometimes ate in the hotel, so I went in to ask them in reception, but I didn't get that far, 'cos I met him coming out.'

'So what happened then?' Alison Knott prompted.

'Nothing much. We went out into the car-park, and I says to him, all polite like, that he'd given me his word of honour as a gentleman that he wouldn't see my Lucy again, and yet I hears as he was.'

'And what did he say to that?'

'He says as how I'm a right stupid berk and as how my Lucy's a right little game bird that likes having her feathers tweaked, and how she ain't too choosy nowadays who does the tweaking. He said that if there was a bit of plucking going, he didn't see why he shouldn't have his share. Only the word he used weren't plucking. That made me see red, it did. Well, I tell you, it ain't no fun hearing that your only daughter's acting like the village whore, even if you know that is what she's been doing.'

Stilito's face looked so helpless that for a moment Alison Knott thought he was going to burst into tears.

'It ain't been easy being a dad all these years,' he went on. 'She were such a pretty kid, and all the boys, and some men as ought to know better, flocked round her like wasps round a jam pot. All I ever wanted was to see her happily married to some good bloke as would look after her and give her lots of kids. I don't know where I went wrong, really I don't.'

'She's young yet, she's only seventeen, Mr Stilito. There's plenty of time for her to have her fling before she meets the right chap, and settles down,' Alison suggested sympathetically.

Stilito didn't seem to have heard her. 'I reckon it was the wife, meself. She'd never smack Lucy when she were a kid, no matter how bad she was. All she ever said to her was, "I'll tell your dad on you when he comes home." It weren't long before she could twist her mum round her little finger and it was left to me to try to give her a bit of discipline and learn her what's right and wrong. I tried reasoning with her, shouting at her, even a few taps with me belt when she was older, but it didn't do no good. Now she hates me. Me, who only wants the best for her.'

'So what did you say next to Fitzpatten?' Reg said firmly, wanting to get back to the purpose of the interview.

'What, him? Oh! I got angry like. "If you don't leave her alone," I shouted, "I'll bloody well shoot you where it hurts most." "Try it," he says. "If you come round here with either your twelve bore or your .22, I'll wrap the bloody barrels right round your thick skull. Go home and have a cold shower, and leave me alone," he says. Then the bugger went off, and left me standing there feeling a right bloody fool, but what else could I have done for my little girl? I tried, didn't I? I ain't big enough to belt him one, or I would'ave.'

'Which direction did Fitzpatten go?'

'Towards his place, of course.'

'What time was that?'

'I don't know. It were after nine. Quarter past or half past. Something like that.'

'Was there anyone else in the car-park who might have seen all this?'

'I don't know. I was so mad I didn't think to look round. I just got in the Land Rover and drove off, but I hadn't gone far when

I see Susan Middlemarch pushing her bike down the road with a flat back tyre. She works in the kitchens there of an evening, she does. I'd cooled down by then, so I puts her bike in the back and gives her a lift home. She lives with her mum on the council estate near Harston,' Stilito explained.

'Right, so she'll be able to confirm the time you left the car-park, will she?' Reg asked. It was wise to confirm a positive statement like that with a direct question. People often told a false story hoping it wouldn't be checked.

'Yes! If you ask her.'

'So you gave her a lift to where she lives. When you left her did you go straight home?'

'Yes!'

'What time did you get home?'

'Don't know for sure. Elevenish, or thereabout. I don't keep looking at me watch all the time, you know.'

'That late? What were you doing all that time?' Reg demanded.

'Delivering me garden stuff, of course.'

'I see. Now, you say you've a .22 rifle, as well as a twelve bore shotgun. Are they both properly licensed?'

'Of course they are. I belong to a rifle club, and I've got them in a proper gun cabinet.'

'We'll need to take your rifle away, to do some tests, you understand. You'll have to leave someone else here in charge while we go and get it. I want it now, right away,' Reg said finally.

Stilito was the last person known to have seen Fitzpatten alive, and he had a pretty fair motive for killing him, together with the means by which a .22 calibre bullet could be impelled into his brain. If ballistics tests showed that the fatal bullet came from that rifle, then it was highly likely that John Frederick Stilito could find himself facing a murder charge.

'It would help if we knew for certain what time Fitzpatten was killed,' Alison Knott mused as she and Reg Finch drove away from the garden centre with the old .22 bolt action rifle in its protective leather case.

'The pathologist said between eight and ten. We've narrowed that down to somewhere, say, between nine fifteen and ten, but unless we get another sighting, we won't get it much more precise,' Reg suggested. 'Anyway, now we'll see what this Middlemarch woman and her mother have to say; after that we'll come back through the village again, and see if Mrs Stilito has got home, then we can find out from her what time her husband did get in the night before last.'

'Stilito wouldn't have been stupid enough to shoot Fitzpatten in the car-park, Reg, where there might be a dozen or so unseen witnesses; but he could easily have got his rifle from the Land Rover and caught up with Fitzpatten near his front door, where the shrubs make it more secluded. He could have shot him there, hidden his body behind the bushes—'

'Then come back later when all was quiet, to bury the body in the bunker,' Reg interrupted. 'I had thought of that, but it doesn't explain the visit of the National Front thugs, does it? Never mind, let's see how Stilito's alibi stands up before we get too involved.'

'We'd better get a move on then, Reg. If it doesn't stand up, we'll need to reinterview the hotel guests for sightings of what was happening in the car-park rather than what was going on on the eighteenth green, and have you thought that Stilito might have used that Land Rover to move Fitzpatten's body down nearer to the bunker? That might have left some traces, so we ought to get Forensic to check it out pretty quickly. We're going to look right Charlies, if Stilito has it steam-cleaned or sets fire to it before we take any action.'

'I'm driving as fast as I can, Alison. We won't get anywhere if we panic.'

Susan Middlemarch was a plump, middle-aged, fair-haired woman with a vague face, big lips and an awfully dry complexion.

'Yes, that's right, sir, John Stilito did give me a lift home. I had a flat tyre on my bike and he saved me a long walk. He's such a nice kind man, he is. It's upset him good and proper, about his Lucy, you know. It's such a shame. He was telling me—'

'What time did you get home, Miss Middlemarch?' Reg interrupted.

'He was telling me how that nasty Fitzpatten man has been leading his little girl into sin—'

'What time did John Stilito get you home, Miss Middlemarch?' Reg Finch insisted impatiently.

Susan Middlemarch frowned and glowered at her questioner. 'Oh, I don't know. Tennish, something like that.'

'Tennish?' Alison exclaimed. 'You said that it was only about twenty past nine when he gave you a lift. It wouldn't take forty minutes to get from there to here. Five more likely. So where did you go in the meantime?'

'He had some paving slabs to deliver to one of the houses down Cromwell Lane. That made him thirsty, so we popped into the Coach and Horses. I don't drink, myself, so I just had a lemonade to keep him company. I told him he shouldn't worry about his little girl, you know. "The good Lord has ways of dealing with them that leads the innocent lambs into sin. Them that does evil, dies by evil," I said, and that's just what has happened to that wicked Fitzpatten, isn't it? It's the avenging hand of God.'

'So, he left you at about ten, did he?' Reg asked hurriedly.

'I never said that,' she protested. 'Tennish it was when we got home here, it were gone eleven when he left.'

'So, what was he doing for that time?' Alison asked.

'Well, first he mended the puncture for me. Me mum was in bed and asleep then, of course. But that didn't take him long. He's ever so clever, he is.'

'And then?' Reg prompted.

'And then,' Susan Middlemarch cocked her head up and looked at him defiantly, 'I gave him one of Mum's bottles of Guinness, got him sat down on the settee and let him tell me all his troubles. He needed someone to talk to, poor chap. He don't get much love or understanding at that home of his. Would you believe it, he cried on my shoulder, so he did. It were my Christian duty to comfort him in his hour of need. So I did, and it ain't no concern of yours just what we got up to.'

'I don't know what time it was when he got home, sergeant,' Mrs Stilito exclaimed with a shake of her head. 'He sleeps in the spare room these days, you see. I know I went to bed about eleven. He didn't wake me up when he come in.'

*

Amanda Knightly drifted slowly into wakefulness. Her first conscious feelings were of being warm, unusually relaxed and very comfortable. It took a few more moments to realise that she lay within the loosely entwined embrace of another body. It was not an earth-shattering experience, there had been lovers before. What was of concern was that for a very long time she had deliberately chilled off all male approaches, but now one had breached her defences. She ought to feel hostility to the man whose arm lay on her stomach and whose chest was crushing one breast, yet she did not. On the contrary, she felt as though a great burden had recently been lifted from her brain, leaving her feeling free and wonderfully alive. There was a muddled dream of having woken to one of the moments that those who sleep alone most dread, when fiery desires build up inside and there is no way they can be properly quenched, but last night a man had come to her need, and brought her peace. The loneliness might return, but at the moment she felt like wallowing in this unrestrained freedom. She could feel the man's nakedness against her flesh, and those fiery passions were building up again within her, but there was no need to fear their torment now. Unashamedly, she stirred the man beside her into life, then lay back to enjoy every moaning and groaning moment as he whirled her senses into a maelstrom of uninhibited pleasure.

'Well, Robin Sainsbury, you're certainly making up for lost time, aren't you?' she whispered later, as she nipped his ear gently between her teeth. The reply was more kisses, but she ignored those and slipped out of the bed and deliberately stood where he could see her in her complete nakedness. Men were so fickle, but this one seemed steady and reliable. He had nice eyes too, and they stared at her body with such awe and admiration that surely he would not leave her to become cold and lonely again.

'Even you can't do it again so soon, Romeo, so how about a game of golf instead?' she suggested brightly.

'Good Lord, I'd forgotten about the tournament. Are you sure you feel well enough?' Robin asked as he swung his feet out of the other side of the bed, and then sat there looking down at his discarded clothes lying on the floor, all creased and crumpled.

85

'I'll manage, just so long as we don't have to play the eighteenth,' Amanda replied determinedly.

'That's fine, then,' Robin said, and he hurried into the bathroom. He was fortunate to find a throw-away razor in the cabinet, so he could make himself reasonably presentable. There was also a change of clothes in the boot of his car, a necessary precaution for someone whose work left him vulnerable to the occasional soaking by an unexpected shower. If he was bewildered by having been so suddenly plunged into an intimate relationship with a virtual stranger, he gave no signs of it, but perhaps he was already concentrating on the coming round of golf.

They arrived on the course with a few minutes to spare.

The wind was a little stronger than it had been the day before, and there were more white puffy clouds scudding along to mask the sun occasionally and make it feel a bit cooler.

Robin and Amanda, with their three-stroke lead over their nearest rivals, were the last to tee off.

Their round did not start very well. Amanda set about playing with a laudable concentration and a determination to apply the advice of her professional partner. Unfortunately that seemed to drive away the element of luck.

A less hurried swing at the first hole resulted in the ball going in the desired direction, but not far enough. A chip and run ran too far, and then she three putted. Their opponents, and Robin, each made effective pars, and so their lead was down to one stroke, on only the first hole.

That stroke disappeared on the second hole. So the last pairing of the tournament were now all square.

It was a bad start for Amanda Knightly and Robin Sainsbury, but many of those ahead fared worse, so it was already looking likely that the tournament winners would be one of the final pairings.

Having evened up the scores and given Amanda and Robin a good old fright, Lady Luck decided to take a hand again. On the next hole they rallied and played much better. It was their opponents' turn to suffer from nerves or over-confidence, and it was they who dropped a stroke.

On the fourth, Amanda twitched on her putting, and again they were all square.

This was the sort of contest that spectators relish. It was becoming as bloody a battle as you could get without gore. Applause,

86

shouts, groans or jeers now greeted each stroke, and the seriousness of every shot was expressed by the grim determination on the faces of the two rival professionals. All their wisdom, skill, and experience were being applied in the desperate business of trying to gain a birdie or save a par, and the result was some excellent golf to thrill the watchers.

Robin's desire to win and to support Amanda's fluctuating game was causing him to play with less caution than usual, and that had led him into some trouble from which he'd only managed to escape by pulling off some spectacular shots.

The lead swung from one pair to the other, and so it was perhaps inevitable that they should be all square with one hole, the final hole, the seventeenth, to play.

Amanda and the other amateur tied the hole, both of them putted up close from a long distance and holed out. That left the battle to be decided by the two professionals.

Robin braved the yawning bunkers from a grassy lie and went for the pin, but he did not get the back spin to stop the ball dead, and it rolled on for nine or ten feet, to leave him with an awkward downhill putt. His opponent had played safe and was twenty feet away from the hole on a line with very little borrow. A line which he read to near perfection. The crowd were convinced his ball was going in, but the cheers turned to groans as it ran out of steam six inches from the hole.

Robin watched grimly as his opponent tapped in. Now he was left with a difficult putt for an outright win. Two putts would mean a sudden death play-off over those opening holes, but if he missed and rolled too far down the slope, he might easily two putt coming back, and then they would lose.

The crowd were silent, but there was a lot of movement as people strove for a better view.

Robin cleaned the ball carefully, then bent to replace it on the green and remove the silvery little coin he used as a marker. The line, he decided, and Amanda agreed, was two inches outside the hole's right lip. He made two practice putts well away from the ball. He must give it only a gentle tap, with almost no follow-through, or else it would race away down the slope. Amanda smiled at him encouragingly as he addressed the ball. For a brief moment he felt light-headedly confident, and that was when he putted the ball. It bobbled along uncertainly at first, veering away from the true line, but then the borrow curled it slowly back in until it came to the edge of the hole and dropped out of sight.

The feeling of euphoria was overwhelming. With the roar of the gallery ringing in his ears Robin Sainsbury grabbed the ecstatic Amanda by the waist and raised her, laughing and utterly delighted, high in the air for the whole crowd to see, as though she were the trophy he'd just won. Then he lowered her to the ground and the pair kissed each other passionately, which brought forth an additional round of applause nearly equal in volume to that which had greeted the winning putt.

Detective Chief Inspector Sidney Walsh and Detective Constable Brenda Phipps had been on their way to review the progress of the search teams that were now ranging through the woods, but had been attracted to the gallery at the seventeenth green by all the activity and excitement.

'That, Chief, is the woman who found Fitzpatten's body in the bunker yesterday,' Brenda Phipps exclaimed as she used his shoulder to support herself while she stood on tiptoe trying to peer over the heads of the crowd in front. 'But she looks a lot different now. She was whiter than a sheet then.'

'I've never seen her look like she is now,' a youngish man nearby said resentfully. 'For two years she's been our company's buyer, and I don't think I've ever seen her smile once. She's not bad-looking, but Lord, she's as cold as an Iceland glacier. I've seen blokes who've tried to chat her up need half an hour's defrosting in the microwave, and they'd still go away worrying about what happens to brass monkeys.'

'She's just won a Wedgwood dinner service, so she ought to be in good spirits, and the chap who's with her doesn't seem to be suffering much from frost-bite, does he? More like an overdose of passion fruit,' Brenda retorted cheerfully.

'I don't know what he's got, but if he's pulled our Amanda, he must have got something, the dirty rotten lucky bastard,' the youngish man muttered grumpily.

7

'If there is a priest-hole anywhere, I'd have thought it was in here,' Reg said, looking round the room that had been Gregory Fitzpatten's study.

'So did we, Reg,' Brenda Phipps replied gloomily, 'but if it is, we can't find it.'

The first impression one had, that the room was small, was, Reg thought, a bit misleading. It was all of fifteen feet long, but narrow, probably no more than seven feet wide, with a leaded window set in that width at the far end, opposite the doorway. Unlike the other downstairs rooms this one had the cross-wise ceiling beams exposed, but the space between them was not the underside of the floorboards of the room above; it had been filled with off-white panels of what looked like modern plasterboard. It clearly had not always been like that, for the beams were pockmarked by the close-set nail holes that had once held up the lathes of an old plaster ceiling. Similarly pockmarked were the three massive upright load-bearing timbers of the outer wall. It all suggested that the restorers of this room had been undecided about which period of the house's history, if any, they should try to re-create, and having stripped away all the inner linings to lay bare the brickwork and the timber frames, they'd given up and left it at that. The inner wall was not original, however. That was an oak-panelled partition of uncertain date, dividing this room from the adjacent one, which was now an ultra-modern kitchen.

'How thick is this inner wall?' Reg asked.

'Not much more than five or six inches,' Walsh replied. 'A simple bit of old-fashioned stud walling, and all the panels are firmly fixed. There are no gaps or movement anywhere.'

Reg looked closely at the outer wall. The timbers were squared-off trunks of oak trees, and the bricks and mortar between were as solid as a rock, so he turned his attention to the desk. It too was of oak, but of no great vintage. He sat down in the modern black plastic cushioned swivel chair and reached down to pull out the bottom drawer of the right-hand pedestal. The space in the plinth beneath was dusty and cobwebby, but empty.

'So is the one the other side. We've checked that, too,' Brenda announced.

'Where haven't you looked?' Reg said in a voice which suggested that in his opinion this looking for secret hiding places in a building that had so clearly been gutted and restored was a complete waste of time.

'We haven't had the floor slabs up. You can do that if you're feeling fit,' she replied with a grin, pointing down to the large grey granite flags.

'I don't think I'll bother just now,' Reg said, then he decided to go into the hall and check out the stairs. Hiding places had been found behind treads and risers that had been contrived as trap doors. Not in this instance however. The stairs were carpeted, and by inspecting the cupboard beneath it was clear there were no obvious spaces or voids. Reg wasn't surprised, but he was saved the necessity of further taxing his brain on a fruitless exercise by the forensic team leader, Dr Packstone, coming into the hall and announcing that he was prepared to give a brief résumé of what his scientific examinations had discovered so far.

'There's nothing of earth-shattering significance, I'm afraid,' Packstone told them when they were all together in the Fitzpattens' sitting-room. 'I'll start with the body. Death, as you know, was caused by a .22 calibre bullet entering the skull cavity from a point below the man's left ear and behind the jaw-bone. The skin round the point of entry was stained by the bullet's propellant smoke, so it was fired at close range, that is to say, within a few inches of the skin. The bullet was deflected and distorted by the inner surface of the jaw-bone, and it then proceeded to ricochet about inside the cranium. Death would have been instantaneous. The pathologist found no other signs of injury, so if the man fell when he died, he didn't crack his head on anything.' Packstone took his dark-framed spectacles off and spent a few moments polishing the lenses with his handkerchief, an action governed more by habit than necessity. 'Now, our examination of the man's clothes is quite interesting. The back of the man's sweater, and also the lumbar region of the jeans he wore, had on them quite a large number of untrimmed fibres from a sheepskin fleece, presumably the hearth rug which you say is missing from this room. A lot of these fibres are well embedded into the material and there are far too many for them to have come from only a casual contact. We think that the body must have lain on the rug, and then the rug was used as a sledge to drag the body along. That could have created the conditions which would have torn and broken so many fibres. The other reason for the sledge theory is that the backs of the man's arms and legs, which presumably dangled off the rug, have picked up all sorts of muck and debris.'

'Really? Are they soil and grass stains picked up when he was dragged over to the bunker?' Walsh asked. 'There must be some signs, but I'm hanged if I could find them,' he went on to admit ruefully.

'Oh no,' Packstone said hurriedly. 'They're not soil and grass stains. Far from it. Some of it is of a dark mould, which we haven't yet specifically identified, but it's not dissimilar to what you get in a fridge that's been switched off with the door left shut. There's slime, too, some of it powdery dry, and some of it, well, fresher. In addition to those there's traces of rat droppings and a few other substances we might need a micro-biologist to identify for us.'

'Rat droppings? Slimy?' Brenda exclaimed with a puzzled frown. 'He hadn't been dragged down a sewer, had he?'

'Not a sewer carrying sewage, but an enclosed culvert possibly. One that's nearly always dry, perhaps, and only occasionally carries water,' Packstone replied thoughtfully.

'You're not saying that the body was dragged down an underground passage, I hope,' Reg Finch asked sarcastically.

Packstone shrugged his shoulders phlegmatically, but he looked irritated at the implied suggestion that what he'd just said was little short of nonsense. 'It's my job to provide the facts, Reg, how they're interpreted is yours. What I'm saying is that some of the body's clothing has been brought into contact with the kind of substances that only form in moist or damp conditions away from direct sunlight.'

91

'Right! That's pretty specific then. Is there anything else you've learned from the body's clothing, Richard?' Walsh asked quickly. Clearly Reg wasn't happy about being forced by scientific evidence to accept the possibility that this remnant of a once large Tudor building might contain secret places.

'Yes, caught up in the wool of the man's jumper we found some tiny splinters of glass, but I'll come back to those in a minute. I want to finish talking about the golf bunker and the searches we made of the approaches to it first. We've made a number of finds, as you'd expect in an area much frequented by people, but their relevance to this case has yet to be determined, and quite frankly I'm not going to spend a lot of time on them at the moment,' Packstone went on rather formally.

'Among other things, loads of golf balls and tee-pegs,' Brenda said with a grin.

'Precisely,' the forensic scientist acknowledged with a slight smile of his own, 'so I'll move on to our examination of this room and this Tudor wing. Firstly, fingerprints, or lack of them. Nearly all the downstairs door handles had been wiped over with a damp cloth, probably the dish-cloth from the kitchen, because there were traces of washing-up liquid. That includes the three Yale locks – the ones on the front door and back door, and the one in the man's study. The only handles not wiped were the ones on the dining-room door and the rooms upstairs. Now, this is important. The security buttons on both outside door Yale locks were in the up position, making the tongue immovable in the closed position. That means, of course, that those doors could not have been slammed shut, or opened from the outside with a key. We considered the possibility that the two men who forced their way in the next day might have pushed those buttons into those position, but our tests showed that their gloves would have left greasy smudges, and there were none. So you can rule that out. We next looked for a means of exit from inside through a window, but', he said, looking directly at Reg Finch, 'they were all closed and their catches were in place. So there you have your first enigma. Whoever set those Yale lock catches did not go out by either of the two doors, or by a window. I'll leave you each to draw your own conclusions from that.' He glared challengingly at Reg Finch.

92

Reg returned a rueful grin. 'Point taken, Dr Packstone,' he admitted. 'Going back to the missing sheepskin rug: according to Mrs Fitzpatten, that was originally in here, in front of the fireplace. If it was then used to drag Fitzpatten's body away, did it also leave a trail of fibres? That might lead us to the entrance of this so-called secret passage.'

'I was coming to that,' Packstone went on. 'There are a few white fibres in a line from the hearth to the hall, but we've found none in any of the other rooms. The rug would have been fleecy side up, of course, and since the underside is tough and leathery, it's unlikely to leave any traces. It would be only the fleece at the rug's edges that might get caught up in the pile of the carpet or anything rough, but I don't think you should place too much significance on any fibres found in this room. They could have been spread by people's feet, and whoever did the cleaning might have dragged the rug across the floor to give it a good shaking outside.'

'This business of a secret passage, though, Richard. You're saying it must exist, because there's no other logical explanation, but we've already been looking for a secret hiding place for the manuscript of a book Fitzpatten had been writing, and we can't find one. Have you any suggestions?' Walsh enquired.

'If you've already looked in the most obvious places, there's little else you can do except strip the panelling from the walls and have all the stone flags up,' Packstone suggested ruthlessly.

'This is a Grade One listed building,' Reg Finch warned. 'I don't think we ought to set about pulling the place apart without at least consulting the council's historic buildings department.'

'Well, you'd better get in touch with them then, Reg. Maybe they can help us,' Walsh said, now looking a little exasperated.

'I can spare a chap with some surveying experience for a few hours, if you like, Sidney,' Packstone offered. 'He could do you an inch perfect plan of the place, inside and out. That might show some variations in the wall thicknesses where any nooks and crannies might be.'

'That might help. Yes, let's have him, please, but, Reg, if you're going to see the historic buildings people you might as well seek out the architects who did the hotel conversion. They must have done a survey of this part of the building as well.'

'Right, I'll do that,' Reg offered, 'after I've seen the hotel manager's wife and daughter.'

'Right! Now you were telling us earlier about glass splinters, Richard?' Walsh prompted.

'Oh yes, the splinters in the man's sweater. Well, we found some more on the carpet in here, and some by the path outside the front door. Our tests show that they are all from the same piece of a very thin glass, the sort you might find in a small photograph frame. The glass is quite brittle, so it's probably several years old,' Packstone explained.

'The two thugs broke the glass of some picture frames, Mr Packstone,' Brenda pointed out. 'Might that account for some of it?'

Packstone shook his head. 'No, they were of a different thickness. I can propose a scenario for you – although speculation, as I've said, is not my province. Fitzpatten may have been holding a small picture frame when he was shot. He would have dropped it, of course, and the glass would have broken, then he must have fallen on it for the splinters to get caught in his jumper. However, that frame is no longer here, so his killer must have taken it away. In which case the killer went out of the front door, and not through a secret passage, because of the other glass splinters that fell on the way down the path.'

Walsh scratched his head and frowned. 'The situation is complex enough as it is. Isn't there anything that you can tell us that might be of some real help, Richard?'

'Not really, not at this stage. There was a small Italian coin under the settee, but I don't know if that's relevant. The ballistics tests on Stilito's .22 rifle will take a few days yet, although a negative result will come through much more quickly than a positive one, and I've sent someone to have a look over his Land Rover. If he finds anything suspicious, we'll bring it in and give it the full treatment. Other than that, whether it's important or not I don't know, but only Fitzpatten and his wife have slept in the bed upstairs, at least since the sheets were last changed.'

'Let me summarise what you're saying, then, Richard,' Walsh said, rubbing at his temples as though his head ached. 'Fitzpatten was probably shot in this room, by someone who went out of the front door, at least for a while. Someone, but not necessarily the same someone, set the Yale lock catches and went round nearly all the downstairs door handles wiping them clean of fingerprints, before dragging Fitzpatten's body away on a sheepskin rug, down some unknown secret passage, which, and

94

I speculate, probably comes out somewhere near the bunker on the eighteenth green, where he was buried. The two hoodlums didn't steal their van until the next morning, so they probably broke in merely to destroy any evidence that remained by putting a torch to the place. The missing manuscript might have been taken by the killer, who may or may not have left behind some glass and a small Italian coin. Is that about right?'

Packstone nodded. 'That just about sums it up,' he said as he got up to leave.

'I find it a bit too confusing at the moment,' Reg Finch admitted ruefully. 'Lucy Stilito said that Fitzpatten was worried that Hitler might be gunning for him because of the book he was writing, yet Mrs Fitzpatten says that it was only about a long-dead hermit. Then a Catholic priest turns up and the music has got to be faced. I don't understand what that's all about.'

'It's only our second day on the case, Reg. You can't expect to make sense of it all yet,' Brenda exclaimed.

'That's right,' Walsh said. 'It's early days. We've got to follow up what we've found out so far, that's obvious, but there's all the staff and guests of a big hotel on our list of possible suspects, so we're going to need a lot of help sifting them out. I'll have a team at headquarters do the investigations into all the people in the hotel and at this golf tournament. They might find that one of them has had dealings with Fitzpatten in the past, and they might find a Catholic priest named Monserrat. We've got enough to do ourselves.'

Mrs Houghton, the hotel manager's wife, was an attractive dark-haired woman with sultry sparkling eyes, who might well have had a large proportion of gypsy blood in her veins, Reg Finch thought. She was a little too tall to be petite, and a little too stout to be elfin, yet the impression was that she was an active sparrow-like person who enjoyed doing – whatever she was doing.

'It's just a matter of form, really,' Reg explained, giving her one of the friendly smiles he used to try and set at ease those he interviewed. 'Would you mind telling me what time your husband arrived home on the night before last?'

'Oh dear, sergeant, I can't do that. I was down at the stables when he got home, looking at Prince. Jo, she's my eldest daughter, thought there was something wrong with one of his hind legs and wanted to call the vet. So I popped down to have a look myself first, and I got talking to Mr Kelly. He's the man who owns the riding school, so it was quite late when I got back,' she explained. 'But Jo was here. She'd know what time her dad got in. She's out taking the dog for a walk at the moment, but she won't be long. Would you like a cup of coffee, or tea, perhaps?'

'A coffee would be very nice, thank you,' Reg replied. It was also very handy, because it would give him the opportunity to talk to her about Gregory Fitzpatten.

'I gather you lived in the hotel when your husband first became the hotel manager. You must have met Gregory Fitzpatten many times,' he said when she came back from the kitchen with two mugs of coffee. The one she handed to him had a picture of Postman Pat on it. Hers had a Tyrannosaurus Rex.

'I met him,' she replied cautiously.

'What kind of person was he?'

Mrs Houghton seemed rather amused by the question, and her eyes smiled boldly back at him. 'Gregory was a charmer. Some men have a way with horses or dogs, with Gregory, it was women.'

'Did he try his charm on you?' Reg asked softly.

The eyes smiled more brightly and she nodded. 'I'm a woman, aren't I? I think I might have been upset if he hadn't. It makes you feel good sometimes, to be chatted up; but he couldn't help what he did, he was made that way. It was the women who took him seriously who were fools. Sex meant no more to him than, well, having breakfast.'

'Did you ever have breakfast with him? And did your husband know?' Reg asked boldly, with what he hoped was an understanding smile.

'The answer to the first question, sergeant, is known only to me and my maker, and I think it would be better if it stays that way. As for Keith, well, he'd be jealous whether he knew or not. It isn't very flattering when someone thinks you're being unfaithful all the time, but that's how it is with him, I'm afraid. Now, that sounds like Jo coming in. Jo! Come in here a minute,' she shouted. 'This gentleman's a policeman, he wants to know what time your father got home the night before last.'

Jo Houghton looked like a normal fifteen-year-old girl in most respects, but usually a young girl's eyes were bright and mischievous; this girl's were icy cold, grey and cynical. She was taller than her mother, though not so pretty, and looked skinny in the tight off-white jodhpurs and long black riding boots.

'That was the night you went down to the stables to check the tendon in Prince's left hind leg, wasn't it? I told you there was nothing to worry about, but you wouldn't listen, would you? Dad came home at something like a quarter to ten. Why do you want to know? You don't think my dad killed Gregory Fitzpatten, do you? Myself, I wouldn't have thought so. Mum stopped running after Gregory years ago, I think. Now, if it had been Sean Kelly down at the stables who'd been murdered, that would be an entirely different matter.'

The silver-haired architect stared down at the drawings he'd spread out on the large table. 'I'll just need to refresh my memory, sergeant. It is quite some time ago; all of twenty-odd years. This is the plan of the building, as it was before we started,' he said, rubbing his chin vigorously, as though that helped his brain's ability to recall past events. 'Yes, and this is the Tudor wing. We did survey it, but we submitted the conversion of that wing into a self-contained, three-bedroom unit, as a planning application for Mr Fitzpatten separate from the one for the hotel. At the time it was just a few old store rooms, with a rear stairway that was rotten and unsafe, if I remember correctly. There were no structural alterations needed, of course, they wouldn't have permitted that anyway. The builders did some of the restoration, such as the new stairs, new roof timbers, and so on, but Fitzpatten did most of the other work himself. I remember we got him a job lot of sixteenth-century linen fold oak panelling from a demolition contractor in the Midlands, but as for hiding places? No! I think you're barking up a gum tree there. There might have been the odd tiny cranny or two in the fireplaces and chimney stacks. You'd expect that in a building of that age. The walls were sound enough, bar the need for a bit of pointing up here and there.'

The photographer shook Brenda Phipps's hand in a limply casual fashion. He was a tall man, with thin reddish hair, dark shadowy eyes, and thick watery lips.

'Yes, indeed. I met Lynda DeMilne that evening, off the seven twenty-five from London. The poor dear was absolutely worn out and shattered. "Your agent's over-booking you," I told her. "You keep this pace up and your face will be old and wrinkled in no time." I didn't like to say she already looked like an old prune, we need all the business we can get these days, but I knew we'd have to work miracles with the lighting, otherwise people would think I'd been taking shots of a ploughed field. Your skin's getting a bit that way too, deary, round your eyes. Anyway, I took her to the hotel, and waited an absolute age while she checked in and unpacked. The things I do for my art. We had dinner, while I took her through the programme for the next morning. Well, I had a dinner, she just had lettuce, nuts and apples. Really boring, it was. Models like her are not fun to be with, they have simply no conversation. Oh, they can switch on the giggles and charm when the men with the big fat wallets are about, but humble photographers like me aren't worth the effort of being nice and pleasant. I was gone by nine, and glad of it. She said she was going to get an early night herself, but if she did it didn't do her much good. Next morning, when I was all bright and bushy tailed, she looked rough – and ducky, when I say rough, I mean rough.'

'I'm sorry,' the Nottingham hotel manager said politely and condescendingly to Brenda Phipps. 'There is no way we could possibly know if Mrs Fitzpatten went out again that evening. Once they've checked in and collected their key, they don't need to go to the reception desk again. They could go out and come back in a dozen times, and we wouldn't know. I can give you a list of all the taxis and local car hire firms, though, if that will be of any help.'

'She's all right, but she looked a bit washed out last night,' Sidney Walsh replied to the big, burly, red-faced Chief Constable's enquiry about Gwen's progress after her operation.

The CC nodded understandingly. 'Some of them are jumping around like spring lambs within twenty-four hours, regardless of the stitches, others take a lot longer. Still, the worst is over now, and she can't be in a better place than Addenbrooke's, can she?' he went on knowledgeably.

Walsh acknowledged the rhetorical question with a short jerk of his head. The trouble was that these pleasantries offered by well-meaning acquaintances were not reassuring at all. The thought kept coming to his mind that if the biopsy showed the presence of malignant cancer cells, then in spite of chemotherapy and drugs Gwen might be one of the statistical medical failures. The vision of a future of empty loneliness was awful to contemplate. It did not help to realise that part of his deep concern for her was contaminated by the selfish thoughts of the gulf she might leave in his life.

'Well, how are things going?' the CC demanded, looking down at his watch to clearly indicate that to him time was precious.

'As well as can be expected, but with this one there's a plague of different possibilities. In his spare time the dead man was the local Don Juan, so there's a few unhappy husbands and fathers about. In addition to that he was an historian and writing a controversial book, the manuscript of which we cannot find, about a hermit priest, which was going to upset Hitler, of all people, according to one of those we've interviewed. Add to that two National Front thugs, a possible secret passage, and a clearly unwelcome visit from a Catholic priest with the improbable name of Father Monserrat. Top that up with a hotel full of guests, and you have all the ingredients for a bowl of real Irish stew, or a crazy cryptic crossword.'

'Hitler's body was found in a bunker in Berlin, Sidney, and he was shot in the head too, just like Fitzpatten. The only difference is that Hitler shot himself, in case the poison he'd taken didn't work. Do you think there's anything in that?'

Walsh's eyebrows went up a few notches in surprise at that bit of wild speculation. The CC often showed signs of wishing he could get out from behind his big administrative desk and involve himself directly in what seemed to many outsiders just a glorious Agatha Christie plot. Well, he could get involved if he liked, Walsh thought. 'I have a gut feeling that the Catholic priest, Monserrat, might know the answer to that, if we could find him. Have you any Church contacts who might be able to track him down?'

The CC looked thoughtful, and pulled at his chin with two fingers. 'I might have. The Church has the equivalent of the Army Lists, if you can get at them, but everything is top secret, of course, that's the way the Catholics work. It'd be easier if they'd got them on computer, but I don't suppose that will happen for another five hundred years. I'll have a go. What else do you know about this Father Monserrat?'

'Nothing, other than the fact that four days ago he was due to visit Fitzpatten. Now, I want to set at least a dozen of the HQ staff on to investigating all the guests and hotel employees, and anyone else who was about when Fitzpatten was killed. Most of it will be a waste of time, but they might just find that one of them had past contacts with the dead man, when he was at the university, perhaps. There's also a photograph album chock full of pictures of girls he'd probably had affairs with. It only mentions Christian names, but if we can locate a few of them, it might help.'

'Your wife is coming on very well, Mr Walsh,' the nurse at the hospital said with a slight professional smile. 'She's been out of bed today, and been walking to the toilet on her own. It's giving her a bit of pain to pass water, but that's normal after an operation like that. It'll go in a few days. Other than that, she's healing well. The consultant was quite pleased when he saw her this morning. No, there's nothing down here about the biopsy report. They do take a few days usually, but they'd go to the consultant first anyway. If you want to talk to him you can make an appointment with his secretary. You've got the number, have you?'

Gwen's eyes brightened as he bent to kiss her. 'Oh, I do love you,' she whispered, her smile wrinkling her snubby nose.

'What, with all these young virile doctors about? We'd better get your eyes tested,' Sidney said with a grin.

Certainly she looked a lot brighter and more cheerful today. She had very little colour to her skin and was obviously still very weak, but clearly she was better than the day before.

He told himself as he left that he wouldn't be worried about her at all, if he knew that the biopsy reports would be negative, but since he didn't, he was worried, and as a result, he worried himself into another lonely night of restless tossing and turning.

*

'I got your message, and I've come, but I really don't know why I've bothered. I can't see what on earth you can have to say that is a "matter of life and death". Really I can't,' the woman said with a frown, looking around the man's sitting-room with an expression more of disdain than curiosity.

'You can sit down. There's no extra charge,' the man said hesitantly, looking nervous and ill at ease.

'I'll stand, thank you. Now, what's all this about?' she demanded haughtily.

'Well, I had the police here yesterday, asking me questions.'

'So?'

'They wanted to know if I'd seen anyone going into the Elizabethan wing on the night Gregory died.'

The woman turned to stare coldly at his face. 'So? And had you?'

'Now I thought you'd be interested in that,' the man said, nodding his head wisely. 'As a matter of fact, I told them I hadn't, but I'm thinking – only thinking, mind you – of telling them tomorrow that, on reflection, I did actually see someone.'

'So? What's that got to do with me?' she asked icily.

'Quite a lot – if I tell them it was you I saw going to the front door. Things could get rather awkward for you, if you see what I mean.'

There was silence for some moments as that statement was mentally digested, then her frown deepened. 'I can't stop you telling a pack of lies, if that's what you want to do,' she replied eventually.

'But I wouldn't be telling lies, would I? Now I've done you a whole heap of favours already. You were very careless, but I've done my best to cover your tracks for you. I moved his body from where you left it, and I put it in the bunker where someone would find it eventually. That's really confused the police. They don't know what to think now. So, provided I keep my mouth shut, you'll be perfectly safe, if you've got yourself a decent alibi, and I hope you have. The only thing is, will I keep my mouth shut? I will, I promise you, if we can come to an amicable agreement.'

'An amicable agreement? What sort of amicable agreement?'

101

'Easy. I just want us to become friends – good friends.'

Her frowning face looked puzzled, as if his words had posed a complex problem that needed time to work on and unravel. 'Friends?' she repeated. 'What sort of friend?'

To answer that he went to stand behind her, and nervously ran one of his fingers lightly down the side of her neck. 'A good friend. An understanding friend,' he whispered hoarsely.

She stiffened at the touch of his finger, but seemed stunned or frightened into stillness.

This negative reaction surprisingly seemed to encourage the man, for he then slowly unzipped the back of her thin cotton dress and eased it off her shoulders, allowing it to slip from her arms and fall soundlessly to the floor.

The woman still made no move, so he reached round and, with a sigh, cupped her breasts in his hands.

'If you let me . . . make me happy . . . I'll never tell a soul . . . I promise you,' he murmured earnestly into her ear with a voice that had thickened with passion and emotion.

The woman's face still frowned, but the touch of the man's hands had cleared away all puzzlement. The frown that remained was from the realisation that she'd already let him go too far. To try and stop him now would risk turning his passion into anger and violence. That could mean pain if he used force to have his way, and she was afraid of pain. It was better by far to do nothing and let it run its course. It wouldn't last long. Men were all the same. It was amazing how often they started from behind, playing with breasts, but they never stayed there long. Further down was a barrier garment of filmy lace and in thirty seconds or so he'd be crouching down before her to have that off. They were all the same, and the usual long drawn-out sigh, as if she were different from the other two and a half thousand million women on the planet. He'd start fumbling with his trousers soon.

'I loved Gregory,' she said, hoping to put him off.

'So what? He was a bastard. I think you're wonderful,' the man grunted as he reached out to touch her thighs.

That did make her move. It was partly an instinctive reaction, from having been through similar routines before, but to the man it seemed as though his hands had roused and excited her. She pulled in her stomach, pushed her hips out provocatively,

102

then moved her right foot two feet to one side. For other men that might have been accompanied by a girlish giggle and a sensual rocking of her hips, but that was not the intention this time. That move brought her outstretched hand within reach of the golf clubs leaning against the wall. She took one up, and looked down to see if the man had noticed, but he was red-faced and totally absorbed with what he was doing. The woman raised the club high, then swung it down with all the strength she could manage. The club hit the man just behind the right ear with a sickening thud; he toppled slowly over on his side, and lay quite still.

8

The spell of fine weather was continuing, and there was just enough of an easterly breeze to make the air fresh and invigorating.

This would probably turn out to be one of those days on which Cambridge is seen at its very best. No doubt the day would show other places at their finest as well, but the best of Cambridge is extraordinarily good. It is not merely all those apparently learned and elegant stone and brick buildings, or the narrow winding river frontage, but the whole atmosphere of the place. That must be nearly unique. You don't have to be fey, or hypersensitive, to walk into St John's, King's, or a dozen other colleges, and feel that you've entered a solid and comfortable other-world that's free of all the nonsensical bustle and hassle of modern life. There is an ethereal peace in them, which is physically relaxing yet can stimulate the brain in such a way that one feels almost certain the solutions to many problems could be sought out – if one wished to waste such a lovely day doing so.

It is not really surprising to find, therefore, that on such a morning many of those who work or live in the city get up early, just to have the time to take a pleasant leisurely stroll through the colleges, to soak in that invigorating atmosphere and prepare their minds for the day's work ahead.

Neither is it very surprising that two of those people might know each other, and meet up where Pembroke Street joins Trumpington Street, at ten minutes to eight in the morning.

'Good morning, professor,' Detective Chief Inspector Sidney Walsh exclaimed, with as much cheerful breeziness as he could muster after yet another near sleepless night. In his light brown suit he looked more like a company executive than a policeman.

'It certainly is a lovely day, isn't it?' Professor Edwin Hughes

104

replied with a beaming smile. He was an elderly, rotund man, of short stature, whose occupational role in life could only be guessed at, probably wrongly, by considering the garments he wore. Sandals, pale blue jeans and a startlingly bright tartan shirt might have been the garb of an Australian opal miner, an eccentric millionaire or a well-dressed tramp, rather than of a Cambridge don.

'I had intended to come and see you some time,' Walsh admitted, his thoughts for the day having already become focused upon the man whose body had been found dead in the sandy golf bunker.

'That, I might hazard a guess, could be about the untimely death of young Gregory Fitzpatten,' Hughes remarked shrewdly. 'Now I hope you'll forgive me if I'm being rude or speaking too bluntly, but your face is showing signs of stress. When we see that sort of thing on our students' faces, we advise them to take a short break fairly promptly, since delay can allow a minor problem to become a major one. Naturally, I make the point to a man of your experience simply because I know that when one is very busy, stress can build up to dangerous levels without one being aware of it.'

Walsh's face twitched at being on the receiving end of such a homily, but it was difficult to feel offended.

'Thank you for the warning. I shall keep an eye on it. Yes, it was about Gregory Fitzpatten. We found a photograph of you with him, in an album. I thought perhaps that you might know the family,' Walsh explained.

'I see,' Hughes said thoughtfully. 'Well, as we're going the same way let's walk together on the sunny side of the street, and if you're not in too much of a hurry perhaps we might find time for a cup of coffee.'

'That sounds like a good idea,' Walsh responded cautiously. Certainly he had intended to come and talk to the professor about Fitzpatten's past life, but not yet, there were quite enough other lines of enquiry to be followed up first. Still, it would be foolish not to hear what this wise old man had to say. Hopefully it would not take too long.

'Adrian Fitzpatten, he was Gregory's father, and I were contemporaries here, at the university. He was a year or so older than I, but we met up at the archery club and became quite chummy for a while. He was reading natural sciences – physics, if I remember rightly – while he was here, but when he'd got his degree he went into law. Our paths crossed only occasionally after that, but when his son, young Gregory, came up to the university, I was asked to keep an eye on his well-being. As, of course, I have done for the sons and daughters of many of my old acquaintances,' the professor explained.

'What sort of boy was he?' Walsh prompted.

'Immature, I'm afraid. He was reasonably intelligent, but in many ways he was childish; much too ready to indulge in the kind of activities the unsophisticated mind considers to be exceptionally humorous and particularly shocking to the older generation. Spontaneous high spirits are one thing, but Gregory's seemed to me to be arranged to bring him into the limelight, for little reason other than the fact that he enjoyed being there.'

'It sounds to me as though you didn't like him very much,' Walsh suggested.

Hughes shrugged. 'I suppose that's true, but when he wished to be, he could be quite charming. Unfortunately, I had already detected the element of insincerity in his behaviour which marred my opinion of him.'

'Was he as interested in women while he was in college, as he appears to have been later on?'

'I imagine so. It was like putting the fox in with the chickens. As I say, he had charm, the good looks to go with it, and no consideration at all for the effect he had on his victims. For that's what they were, victims. The ability to pass exams does not equip a young lady to deal with predators like him, and there were many who suffered deep emotional problems, and a few attempted suicide.'

'He took a degree in history, I believe,' Walsh said conversationally. Hughes was merely confirming what was already known, and it did not seem likely that he would be the source of any new information. 'Since then he has been writing books. His latest, according to one report, was supposed to be about Hitler, yet his wife told us that he'd been collecting material about the life of a Hieronymite priest who died in the 1930s.'

They may have been conversational words, but they had the effect of causing the smile to abruptly leave the plump professor's normally cheerful face.

'Hitler? Hieronymite priest? That prompts an interesting association of ideas.' Hughes frowned thoughtfully. 'The newspaper said that Gregory had been found shot in a golf bunker. Where was he shot? Whereabouts on his body, I mean?'

'Here. Just below the left ear.' Walsh pointed to the place on his own neck with a finger of his left hand. 'The bullet went up into his brain. Death must have been instantaneous.'

'Oh dear,' the professor exclaimed grimly.

'Why? What do you mean?'

Hughes shook his head reluctantly. 'I need to refresh my memory, inspector, or rather confirm my memory. In fact, I think a word with George would be the wisest thing for us to do.'

They had crossed the road and entered into the grounds of Downing College by then, but instead of heading for his own rooms, the professor ushered his guest towards the college library.

In there the professor looked round expectantly, then led the way to a table at which sat a heavily jowled man with tight wavy grey hair and a long hooked beak of a nose.

'George, I'd like you to meet Chief Inspector Walsh. George is an authority on modern European history, inspector,' Hughes explained. 'George, a man's body was recently found in a bunker, a golf bunker it's true, but nevertheless a bunker, and he'd been shot in the head, here, under the jaw. Now, according to one account the dead man had been writing a book about Hitler, according to another, he was writing about a Hieronymite priest who died in the 1930s. Does that little scenario suggest anything to you?'

George's cool grey eyes studied Walsh's face for a moment, then he spoke quietly in a voice surprisingly as deep as Paul Robeson's, yet as gruff as Louis Armstrong's. 'Do sit down, inspector. I've heard about you and the things you get up to, from Edwin here. Is he playing one of his little games, or is he being serious?'

'Serious, I think,' Walsh ventured with a slight smile.

'In which case, I'll be serious too. If your man committed suicide in the same manner as Adolf Hitler, in a golf bunker, then I'd merely suggest to you that he was insane, and that you're wasting my time,' George announced flatly.

'We don't think he committed suicide,' Walsh responded doubtfully.

'Well, that's different. I'll carry on then. It's the "Hieronymite" reference that's interesting. There was a Catholic priest who was a member of the Hieronymite order of hermits, and who died in the 1930s, in Germany, and his name was Bernhard Stempfle. Father Bernhard Stempfle, to give him his common title, if you can live with the ultimate insult to human intelligence of calling a man who has voluntarily accepted a life of celibacy "Father". I'm a Jew, so I can say things like that. I've no fear of being consigned to a Catholic hell. Hieronymite means, by the way, that he was a member of one of a number of small hermit orders established in the thirteenth and fourteenth centuries. Bernhard Stempfle was the editor of an anti-Semitic newspaper in the town of Miesbach, but more importantly, he was an adviser and mentor to Adolf Hitler. It was Stempfle who edited, and some say actually wrote most of, Hitler's *Mein Kampf*, which was published in the summer of 1925. There is little doubt among scholars that Stempfle greatly influenced the development of Hitler's anti-Semitic attitudes and ideas, which, as you must realise, eventually resulted in the Holocaust.'

'A Catholic priest? Involved with the leader of Nazism? Would the Pope have allowed that?' Walsh asked, wondering just what all this had to do with the case he was investigating.

George shrugged his shoulders. 'Nobody knew then where Nazism would lead. There is much in the Church's attitude at the time which suggests it wanted to see a strong united Germany, as a bulwark to any threat from the big Red Bear, Russia, which was, of course, anti-Christian. Stempfle may have been allowed to help promote Hitler's quest for power with that in mind. In the wider political field the Church would have encouraged any country that was prepared to attack and defeat Stalin's Russia, simply to free the Christians there. Ironically, the man who would later pull the Vatican's political strings was already in Germany. The future Pope Pius XII – Archbishop Eugenio Pacelli – was the Apostolic Nuncio to Germany in the 1920s. He must have known what Stempfle was up to, and one must suppose he approved, or else he would have stopped it.'

'Hold on a minute. If Stempfle was helping Hitler to achieve power in Germany, was he also helping Hitler to form his plans of what to do with that power if he got it?' Walsh asked with a frowning look that margined on disbelief.

'Possibly.'

'And that was with this future Pope's blessing?'

'Knowledge, was all I said. Blessing? Who knows? Pacelli was recalled to Rome in 1929, and was elected Pope in 1939.'

'Hitler's future plans obviously included the wholesale murder of millions of Jews—'

'And other races and religions,' Hughes interrupted.

'Inspector,' George said, wagging a finger knowingly, 'if you could only half prove that Stempfle was acting with the full approval of the future Pope Pius XII, you'd have all the ingredients for a pretty sensational book. Pius might have been good at politics, but he was lousy at understanding world opinion, or else he didn't care a damn about it. He refused to directly condemn the extermination camps, and certainly did nothing to stop them. Later, when he said that what had happened brought to his mind pictures of Revelations' Last Judgement, it merely gave the impression to the world that he thought the Jews had been consigned to the fiery furnaces of hell a little sooner, rather than later.'

'Historians must have found out all there was to know about this Stempfle by now. If the story was there, it would be public knowledge, surely?' Walsh said, frowning deeply.

'Not so. The time came when Stempfle had outlived his usefulness, and he was disposed of in Hitler's purge of 1934. His body was discovered in the woods outside Munich. The official line given out was that he'd been shot while trying to escape. Meanwhile Hitler's secret police had raided the place where he lived and destroyed all his documents. There's nothing left for historians to find,' George explained with a condescending smile.

'But Mrs Fitzpatten said that she and her husband had spent days in Rome and other places seeking out the old letters and correspondence of priests who were in the Hieronymite order during the thirties,' Walsh said, still looking a little bewildered.

'Did she now? But was Stempfle the priest about whom Gregory Fitzpatten was really making enquiries? You're keeping us on unnecessary tenterhooks, inspector,' Hughes said accusingly.

Walsh absent-mindedly drummed his fingers on the table top. 'I don't know,' he admitted lamely.

'You don't know? But surely you've got Fitzpatten's notes and manuscripts? Haven't you read them?' Hughes demanded urgently.

'We can't find them. We've searched everywhere. We've even sunk to the level of looking for a priest-hole or secret passage . . .'

'And have you not found it?' Hughes asked quietly. Dancing devil lights now appeared to sparkle in his clear brown eyes.

Walsh looked at him hard, and then shook his head ruefully. 'Do you know where it is?' he asked with a reluctant smile.

Hughes nodded enthusiastically. 'Well, I know where one priest-hole was. Adrian showed it to me when I spent a weekend there once. It was a long time ago, of course, but you don't forget things like that. The whole place was nearly a complete ruin then, but it's a hotel now, I understand. I've never been back.'

'Was there a secret passage connection too?'

'Yes, indeed there was, but we never explored it, because Adrian's father had set a heavy steel grid over the entrance. Apparently the tunnel wasn't safe.'

'Professor, I know you're a busy man, but would you please come out to Hasling Abbey and show me where those places are?' Walsh requested formally.

'I thought you were never going to ask,' Hughes said with undoubted delight. 'George, I've got a tutorial in half an hour. You will stand in for me, won't you, old chap?'

'Sod you, Edwin. Why can't I come too? Oh, all right, but if you find any of Stempfle's letters you must treat them like gold dust, and let me have them straight away. They'll be important history, and absolutely vital for our understanding of the politics of the period.'

'I'm glad you didn't ask George to come with us, inspector,' Hughes said quietly when he'd made himself comfortable in the passenger seat of Walsh's car. 'I don't think it would be wise for him to see Stempfle's letters, if they exist.'

'You're not suggesting that we withhold a vital piece of historic evidence, just because it might prove something that some people might not want proved, are you, professor?'

'Not for that reason, specifically, inspector, but would you approve of pulling the pin out of a hand grenade, just to prove

110

it's live, or pressing the nuclear button just to prove the bombs will work? That's what the effects would be like, believe me. Hitler was a Catholic, you see, and the Jews have every right, in my opinion, to feel mighty aggrieved at the way they were treated, but we're fifty years on now, and things have settled down, to a large degree. All that Stempfle's letters would do is to stir up the passions and the hatred all over again. Let's hope that the Vatican doesn't know what Gregory was up to, because they wouldn't be too happy about it either. Whatever the truth is about Pius XII, such revelations could shake the faith of the faithful, and they wouldn't want that.'

'That's one of the things that has been worrying me, professor,' Walsh admitted. 'I think the Vatican might know. A priest was due to visit Fitzpatten the other day, and when he told his wife about it he said that he'd got to face the music some time or other. Just how far would the Church go to prevent the faith of the faithful being shaken?'

'That I would not like to give an opinion on. Of course, Gregory's killer might have taken all his papers.'

'Yes, but I don't think so. The Tudor wing was broken into the morning after he was killed, by some National Front thugs who were planning to set fire to the place. We stopped them just in time, but if the killer couldn't find what he was after, setting a torch to the place later might be the next best thing.'

He was interrupted by the bleeping of his car phone.

'Chief?' came Brenda Phipps's voice above the sound of clicks and atmospheric cracklings. 'We've got some interesting developments. Houghton, the hotel manager, didn't go home last night. They found his car down at the stables in the village, early on this morning, and now they've found him too, under a load of straw bales. He'd been bashed on the back of the head, apparently.'

'Is he dead?'

'No, but they've called an ambulance to him, and Reg has gone down to have a look round.'

'Tell him I'll meet him there, Brenda.'

'Hold on. I haven't finished yet,' Brenda continued quickly. 'Stilito didn't go home last night either. I've just got back from seeing his wife. He's packed all his clothes and apparently drawn all their savings out of the building society. He's not turned up at work, so I think he's done a bunk, Chief.'

111

'Meet me at the Tudor wing in half an hour,' Walsh instructed, and he put the phone down. 'I'm sorry, professor. We'll need to make a short diversion first. One of our suspects was bashed on the head last night, and another seems to have scarpered.'

'Really? How exciting! I do envy you, inspector. You must never be bored.' He sighed. 'My life is very mundane in comparison to yours.'

'Hello, professor. This is a surprise. It's nice to see you again,' Reg Finch said with a rather puzzled smile.

'The professor knows where the priest-hole and the secret passage are, Reg,' Walsh explained briefly.

'Does he indeed? Well, it only goes to show how wrong one can be. I didn't think there was one. Never mind. Well, we've found a torch, boss, so I think Houghton might have been prowling round here last night. Maybe he was expecting to find his wife with this fellow Sean Kelly. Anyway, whoever bashed him was waiting just inside the fodder store room. You can see the tracks made on the floor when he was dragged into the corner, that's where the hay bales were piled on to him, so that he couldn't move. When he came to his senses he probably exhausted himself shouting for help and fell asleep. He was still asleep when they found him. At first he said it was Kelly who attacked him, but then he admitted he hadn't really seen who it was. Kelly lives in the house at the top of the lane, but he's not there. Gone to London on the early train, the woman who cleans for him said.'

'Any sign of the weapon used?' Walsh wanted to know.

'There were several bits of wood lying about that could have been used. I've bagged them all up. Forensic can have a look at them. There's nothing else to do here, so I might as well come up to the hotel with you, and see where this priest-hole is. I can see Kelly, and Mrs Houghton and her daughter, later,' Reg decided.

Sidney Walsh and the professor met up with Reg Finch and Brenda Phipps in the hotel car-park, and they all walked quickly towards the entrance of the Tudor wing, excitedly anticipating Hughes's revelation of the secret places within.

However, there was to be another distraction first.

Outside the front door Detective Constables Alison Knott and Arthur Bryant were engaged in conversation with a tall, spotty youth who had an anxious, worried look on his face.

'What's the problem?' Walsh asked.

It was the spotty youth who responded. 'I'm Mr Myres's assistant at the golf shop, but he hasn't opened up yet. I've rung the bell dozens of times and he still hasn't answered. I can't get in, and there's two people waiting for lessons – well, only one now, the other has stomped off in a rage. He's never been late opening up before, normally he's up with the lark. I'm worried he might have been taken ill or something.'

With one man involved in the murder enquiry having been attacked and another gone missing, the young man's news presented alarming possibilities, so Walsh acted promptly.

'Come on,' he said to all and sundry, and he ran down the path to the golf shop. There, he rattled the locked door, then peered through the windows. 'Are you sure he didn't say he'd be out today?' he grunted.

'Definitely not,' the spotty youth replied confidently. 'Anyway, he was booked to give lessons. He wouldn't have done that if he was going out.'

'Right, then. Stand back,' Walsh instructed. It was only a normal Yale lock, which an expert could open very quickly, but there wasn't time to get one, and delay was unacceptable. The door was glass-paned, so the traditional dramatic shoulder charge was hardly appropriate; what was needed here was a firm kick on the frame, by the lock. The first kick merely loosened screws, it was the third that wrenched them free.

'Brenda, Alison, you come with me. The rest of you, stay here,' he instructed as he hurried across the shop and up the stairs leading to the flat above. There he pulled up short at the sight of the devil-eyebrowed golf professional, Andy Myres, lying prone on the floor of his sitting-room.

'He's still alive – just about,' Alison Knott announced from down on her knees, having fingered for a pulse at the base of the man's neck.

'I'll call another ambulance, Chief, and ask Dr Packstone to send some of his team over,' Brenda said from the doorway.

Walsh nodded, and proceeded to look round the room. There was no sign of a struggle – on the contrary, all looked neat and tidy.

'There's a funny smell in here,' Brenda said, wrinkling her nose. 'It's not you, is it, Alison?'

'Certainly not. I had a bath this morning,' that individual protested indignantly.

'No, silly. It's a perfume of some sort. It's a very faint musky smell,' Brenda went on.

'I can't smell anything at all,' Alison replied.

'Alison, stay here with him until the ambulance and the forensic team arrive. Then come and join us in the Tudor wing,' Walsh said as he went downstairs and outside. 'Mr Myres has had a fall and hurt his head,' he explained to the spotty youth. 'You'd better have the day off. There's nothing you can do here.'

'Was the man who lived here also on your suspect list?' Professor Hughes asked boldly, his natural curiosity betraying him into asking what might be a taboo question.

It didn't seem to bother Walsh. 'No, I can't say he was. Not on my list, anyway.'

'But he might have been on someone else's suspect list,' the professor suggested tentatively. 'Aren't two men being attacked, and another one perhaps being frightened away, a bit too much of a coincidence?'

Walsh smiled wanly. 'I should rather think so, professor. Stilito, the man who appears to have run away, was the last person we know of who saw Fitzpatten alive, and the other two were in the vicinity at about the same time, so they each might have seen something they haven't yet told us about. These attacks might be warnings to them to keep their mouths shut. On the other hand, Stilito might have bashed the other two before he scarpered, or alternatively the murderer has decided to spread out even more red herrings to confuse us. I'd have thought there were enough of those already, but there's little point in speculating yet, because Forensic may find something that will help limit the possibilities, and anyway we must concentrate our efforts at the moment on the main crime – Fitzpatten's murder.'

'Absolutely fascinating,' Hughes commented, nodding his head wisely.

'I think, professor,' Walsh went on, 'it's time for you to reveal the mysteries of the secret places to us. Then perhaps we can find time for a cup of coffee. I'm parched.'

'Everywhere seems so very different,' the professor said doubtfully, looking round the small hallway. 'Anyway, it's upstairs, the room on the south side.'

'Upstairs?' Reg muttered, looking extremely puzzled.

'That's the main bedroom. Come on, professor,' Brenda said, pulling on his sleeve and hurrying him to the stairs.

'This was part of a big sitting-room once. The entrance to the priest-hole was about here,' he announced, indicating a spot on the windowless outer wall. 'It was down near the floor, but this all looks different. There were little carved roses at the intersections, and you had to turn two of them together. Then the panel between, which was hinged at the top, could be pushed in. We wriggled through it backwards and there were iron rungs set in the wall to climb down, to a tiny room below. It's inside the big outside buttress, you see, but this isn't the original panelling. It's all been changed. I'm afraid it rather looks as though it's been sealed up.' He stood and pulled at his fleshy chins thoughtfully, a look of bitter disappointment on his face.

'Now let me think,' he mused. 'There was once another entrance from the room below, but the hinges and mechanism of that door had obviously long since rusted away or disintegrated, because when I was in there, that part of the wall had several wooden planks nailed across it, to hold everything together. What I am certain of is that if Adrian did the restoration here himself, he would definitely not have sealed that hidy-hole up completely. He was much too proud of it. Who wouldn't be, for heaven's sake? It's more precious than a Rembrandt or a Goya. Any fool with money can buy them, but your own private priest-hole is unique. It's history, Adrian's personal family history. You could dismantle this panelling to gain access, but there must be another way in – from the room below, perhaps.'

'That's more like it,' Reg acknowledged hopefully. 'That was Gregory Fitzpatten's private study, with its own Yale locked door, to keep everyone else out.'

'Is that so? Let's go down and see, then.'

The professor stared at the middle section of the outer wall of the study. 'This brickwork seems solid enough, so if there is another doorway, it must be this.' He tapped his knuckle on the massive squared-off tree trunk that was clearly a main part of the load-bearing structure. 'It would be far too heavy to hang on simple top or side hinges. It might rock on a base set pivot, but that would require a complicated counterweight mechanism, or else it would fall over. So, obviously, it must pivot in the middle.' He reasoned aloud. 'A piece of paper, please.'

The paper was inserted into a tiny gap between one side of the wooden post and the brickwork. It could be slid up and down reasonably easily, but there was an obstruction in the middle, and another a foot from the floor, and yet another three feet from the ceiling.

Hughes's eyes were now bright, and his face had regained its cheerful expression. 'A central pivot, and two locking bolts, access to which may well be through two of these tiny nail holes. Is there, in any of the desk drawers, a longish thin rod, with perhaps a flattened end, like a screw driver?' he asked Brenda.

In fact there were two narrow rods of hardened steel, six inches long, and barely an eighth of an inch in diameter. The ends however were not flattened, they had tapered squared tips, and a cross-piece was welded on T-fashion at the other end to give leverage. They fitted two of the false nail holes quite perfectly. When they were turned in an anti-clockwise direction there came a satisfying sound, as of well-oiled bolts being drawn back.

'That's quite clever,' the professor murmured approvingly as he pushed at the bottom half of the massive fifteen- or sixteen-inch wide timber post, and watched it swing inwards, smoothly and silently. Then he had to step back quickly, for the top was coming down, and would have hit him on the head, otherwise.

'There you are, inspector. One priest-hole. Circa 1600, give or take twenty years or so, I should think,' the professor said with a smugly self-satisfied smile.

'Steady on. Stand back. One at a time,' Walsh said quickly. Everyone was trying to squeeze into the gap at the same time.

He shone his torch into the space. There was a step down to a stone floor, so it was easier to go in backwards, but once inside there was plenty of headroom, and there was a light switch screwed to the brickwork.

'It's all mod cons in here,' he said, as he flicked the switch and bathed the tiny room with bright light. Incongruously, taking up most of the space to the right of the entrance, was a modern, green-painted steel filing cabinet. There was nothing else, except a long narrow sheet of thick plywood lying on the floor, which, Walsh discovered when he pushed it to one side with his foot, was covering a hole in the floor, and that hole in the floor had steps going down inside it. With a surprising show of indifference for a one-time Enid Blyton fan, Walsh ignored the hole, and instead pulled open the top drawer of the cabinet. It contained a number of ring-binders full of hole-punched A4 sheets. The second held more papers and computer discs, as did the others.

'Well, it looks as though we might have found Gregory Fitzpatten's notes and manuscripts,' he announced to all the apparently bodiless heads that were peering in, 'but there's rather a lot of it.'

'Someone's got to explore that tunnel, Chief,' Brenda said, her voice husky with urgency. 'If the body was taken out that way, we've got to find out where it goes to as soon as possible.'

'That's true,' Walsh agreed as he stepped back into the study. Even for a man of his size it wasn't difficult, not if he went sideways on and kept his head down. 'There doesn't seem to be a lot of headroom down in the tunnel. Do we have any volunteers?'

'I'll go,' said Brenda Phipps and Arthur Bryant in unison.

'I'm probably a bit too tall,' Reg Finch explained.

'I'm ... er ... quite happy to stay behind if those two want to go so badly,' Alison Knott said, with a slight grimace.

'I'll go, if you like, inspector, but I might have difficulty if the passage gets narrow. I used to be slim and agile once, but like a tree, each passing year seems to have added another ring round my middle,' the professor said with a loud chuckle.

'That's very kind of you, professor, but I think this is best left to the younger ones among us. Besides, I was rather hoping you'd help us read through these papers to find out just what Fitzpatten's book was about.'

Hughes nodded his agreement, but he was by then studying the outer end of the massive pivoted timber intently. 'I think the

117

original bolts must have been in these slots at the side, but I can't see how they were activated. All this new mechanism Adrian has screwed on to the back of the door may be stainless steel engineering perfection, and designed to last for evermore, but it is hardly authentic. I'm not sure I approve of tampering with history to such a degree.'

'If you must come, Arthur, come. We're wasting time. You'd better have Reg's torch,' Brenda interrupted the professor's ramblings impatiently.

'You both ought to wear hard hats and take a rope, perhaps,' Walsh suggested, trying to be practical.

'No way, Chief,' Brenda snapped. 'This isn't a pothole. You needn't worry, I'll go in front, and if it looks at all dangerous, we'll come straight back. We might be able to keep in touch with our radios – anyway, we'll try.'

'All right, but you be careful.' That last remark was addressed to Brenda's back as she disappeared down the steps and into the hole, followed by an eager Arthur Bryant.

'Damn it, Arthur, don't tread on my heels. It's not too bad at all, Chief. It's roofed with stone slabs, and the sides are stone and brick. It's about three feet wide and four and a half feet high. I can walk easily enough, if I bend. It looks safe enough to me. Ouch. We could have done with the hard hats after all, but never mind. I'm going on.'

'Right, I'll pass out all the papers and files, Reg. Take them into the sitting-room where there's more room. You can sort them out in there,' Walsh suggested.

'I think I can be more usefully employed by making some coffee,' Alison announced sensibly, and she wandered off to the kitchen.

Having removed all the papers, Walsh sat on the floor of the little room, with his legs dangling in the passage, to listen to Brenda's radio commentary on the exploration of the tunnel.

'There's another passage coming in from the right, Chief, but we're going straight on because something has definitely been dragged along the floor recently,' she reported. 'It's a bit eerie down here in places, where roots have grown through the gaps between the roof slabs.'

Then a few minutes later: 'We've gone about fifty feet or sixty feet, I'd guess. It's slightly downhill, and there's yet another passage coming in on the left. It looks a bit damper up there, so perhaps it still acts as a drain when it's been raining. There's quite a lot of newish brickwork in places where the walls probably caved in once. Someone's spent a lot of time clearing this main passage, and making it safe. Anyway, we're going on, following whatever was dragged along.'

'It's my turn to lead. Why have you always got to stay in front?' Arthur could be heard complaining.

'Because I have,' Brenda explained with unanswerable feminine logic. 'There's another passage on the right, but it doesn't go anywhere, the roof's fallen in. The air's getting a bit stuffy, but it's still all right.'

It was another five minutes before the radio crackled again, and this time Brenda's voice was much fainter, but clearly very excited.

'Chief, we've found the sheepskin rug, and there are some steps going up. The passage does go on further, but this is as far as the body was dragged, that's for certain. Come down, Arthur. Let me go first. There's a wide ledge at the top, and what must be a stone door, Chief. It's a big granite slab with wires attached to the bottom that go round pulleys and have weights on the other end. Like the counterbalance system on an up-and-over garage door. The slab must have hinges at the top, although I can't see them, and there's a stainless steel bolt on either side. I've drawn them back and I'm pulling on a handle. It's moving slowly. It's a bit stiff, but it's coming.'

There was a faint sound of stone rubbing on stone, and then an equally faint high-pitched feminine scream.

'Brenda! Are you all right?' Walsh shouted in alarm at his radio.

Brenda took no notice of his call. She knew that it wasn't she who had screamed, so she was wriggling on her stomach through the surprisingly large opening. There she found herself on the flagged floor of the old stone summerhouse, looking up at not only the ashen and horrified face of the amateur golfer, Amanda Knightly, who was clearly almost ready to faint herself into yet another decline, but also the frowningly serious face of the professional, Robin Sainsbury.

'This file definitely contains some of Fitzpatten's research papers, professor,' Reg said quietly. 'It's like a long diary of

119

business or social events. Embassy dinners, exhibitions, things like that, and it's got dates down the side from 1925 to 1929, and there are three columns headed "EP", "AH" and "BS", with some ticks in them.'

'You read German, do you, sergeant?' the professor exclaimed with an approving smile as he glanced at the papers in Reg's hands. 'That is very interesting. It does look as though we might be on the right track. "EP" is, I imagine, Archbishop Eugenio Pacelli, Apostolic Nuncio to Germany in the twenties. "AH" should be Adolf Hitler, and "BS", Bernhard Stempfle. These are obviously some of the public events attended by at least two of them, sometimes all three, which young Gregory no doubt intended to use as proof that they had met up in and around Munich or Berlin, and were therefore known to each other. But it was not the public meetings of those three that were important as far as Gregory's thesis was concerned, it was the private ones, the ones held in secret, of which there would be no record kept. What I was hoping we'd find are copies of private letters, written by Stempfle, to some of his friends or colleagues.'

'There are some copies of old letters in that box file on the floor. Some of them are in German, but I can only read a few of the words, because the handwriting is too faded. Others are in Latin or Italian, I think.'

The variety of languages obviously did not deter the old professor. He eagerly took up the tattered box file and pottered back to his armchair by the window, where he took a sip from the cup of coffee Alison had brought him, and then proceeded to browse through the file's contents.

9

'That woman, Amanda Knightly, let out such a screech, Chief,' Brenda Phipps said with a chuckle.

'And Sainsbury went as white as a sheet too. You'd have thought we were a pair of headless ghosts,' Arthur Bryant added from where he sat eating at the Fitzpattens' dining-room table.

'But what were they doing in the old summerhouse? That's still cordoned off, isn't it?' Reg asked.

'Yes, it is. I think they were having a bit of kiss and cuddle. It's all roses and gypsy violins with those two, but they said they were looking for someone to ask if they could use the Man Trap bunker to practise in. Apparently the Knightly woman is still having nightmares about the dead Fitzpatten's hand coming up out of the sand holding her ball. She thinks that the only way she'll ever exorcise that ghost is by spending hours doing bunker shots from there. I told her she'd have to wait a while yet. Sainsbury seemed uncommonly interested in what we were up to though, but perhaps that's not surprising, when someone suddenly appears from under the very seat you're sitting on.'

'Would anyone like another slice of pizza? There's plenty left. HQ have done us proud today,' Alison asked from the dining-room doorway.

'Yes, please,' said the ever-hungry Arthur.

'I think I could manage another piece too, and another cup of coffee, my dear, if it's not too much trouble,' Professor Hughes added from the head of the table. 'Are you sure Mrs Fitzpatten doesn't mind us making ourselves so much at home?'

'That's what she said we could do. Don't worry, we'll leave it all as it should be,' Walsh said reassuringly. 'So what did you do then, Brenda?'

'We went back into the tunnel and closed the slab behind us, there's no way it can be opened from outside, and went to explore the rest of the main passage. It only went another twenty feet or so, and it was completely blocked by a fall,' Brenda went on. 'That meant we had some thinking to do, didn't it?'

'Why?' Professor Hughes asked. 'I would have thought you would have been very pleased with what you had discovered.'

'Oh yes, and so we were, but you don't know that Forensic have said that all the doors and windows in this place were locked on the inside, so we'd expected Fitzpatten's killer to have gone out through the tunnel, but since we found that the stone door to the summerhouse was bolted on the inside, and there's no way those bolts could be shot from the outside, he obviously didn't leave that way.'

'So we went back to explore the other passages,' Arthur explained. 'I think it's all part of the fresh-water end of the Abbey system, Reg, because we didn't see anything that looked like their loos, thank goodness.'

'That's got nothing to do with it, Arthur,' Brenda said. 'So we went up the first tunnel off the main passage—'

'She means the first coming back. It was the second or third going down,' Arthur interrupted helpfully.

'We went up the first tunnel off the main passage,' Brenda went on, ignoring Arthur's correction, 'and that was a bit hairy. The walls looked pretty dicey, in places, and sure enough, that was blocked by a fall. There was no way out there. So that only left the second tunnel off the main passage. That one was in better condition, although it too was blocked by a fall, but it was a good thing we'd got our eyes open, or we'd never have spotted it.'

'Else I wouldn't have spotted it, she means,' Arthur said quietly.

'The stone roof slab before where the tunnel had fallen in wasn't a stone slab at all, it was a big piece of thick waterproof plywood, painted grey. It was a trap door. When I pushed it open, where do you think we were?' Brenda gave no time for answers to that question, because she went straight on. 'In the cupboard under the stairs, in the golf shop.'

There was a short silence which Arthur broke, when he'd swallowed a mouthful of pizza. 'That branch tunnel obviously goes right under the golf shop,' he said. 'I think that when that tunnel collapsed, Myres must have suddenly found himself with a big hole in the floor under his stairs. The tunnel was only about three feet down, so when he dug down a bit he couldn't help but find it. I reckon that Myres tidied it all up in such a way that Fitzpatten would never know that there was suddenly another entrance into the tunnel system. We wouldn't have spotted that painted trap door if we hadn't been looking for something like that, honestly.'

'Why would Myres be concerned about what Fitzpatten thought, Arthur?' Alison asked.

'You might not have noticed, but that secret door in the study can be opened from the inside. All you'd need is a tapered bar to fit those square holes, and you could undo it easily. So Myres would have found that he could get in and out of the Elizabethan wing whenever he wanted to, provided the Fitzpattens were out, of course—'

'We know all that, Arthur,' Brenda interrupted. 'Obviously it was Myres who took Fitzpatten's body out.'

'Yes, but there's another thing you don't know,' Arthur insisted. 'I've been up those iron rungs the professor said were in the walls to where the old moving panel in the bedroom once was. Well, there's a little hole in the panel that's there now, and if you put your eye to it, you can see anything that's going on in that room. I reckon Myres was a peeping Tom, and watched Mrs Fitzpatten getting undressed sometimes. There's no point in the hole being there otherwise.'

'Why should you think that Myres has as dirty a mind as yours obviously is, Arthur?' Brenda said scornfully.

'Myres is probably our killer then, boss,' Reg suggested.

'Not necessarily. What's his motive? And don't forget those glass splinters that Packstone told us about. Someone definitely went out of the front door after Fitzpatten was killed. Nevertheless, it's all very interesting,' Walsh muttered thoughtfully. 'How have you been getting on with Fitzpatten's papers, professor?'

The professor seemed surprised to be asked that question. Research to him was a leisurely pursuit, with plenty of time to ponder, consider and reflect; however, his brain quickly listed some sensible observations. 'I've only had time for a cursory glance at Gregory's manuscripts, inspector, but I must say I'm impressed by the manner of his writing. He can be very convincing. I have much more to read yet, but there is no doubt that Gregory's intention was to announce to the world the proposition that the Catholic Church, through the future Pope and his henchman, Stempfle, had actively assisted Hitler to achieve power specifically so that he would use that power to destroy the enemies of Christendom. As evidence to support this he has six incomplete letters which he purports were written by Stempfle to other members of the Hieronymite order. Let me say, here and now, that in my opinion this evidence is highly dubious. Phrases are taken completely out of their original context, and two of the letters, although signed by a Bernhard, are clearly in a different handwriting to the others. If this book were published, historians would hotly dispute Gregory's claims, but that is not the point. If it were launched in a blaze of publicity the damage would have already been done, with all the problems we talked about earlier today. This book is like an old explosive. It is highly dangerous, and it should be handled with great care, and preferably destroyed at a distance by means of a remotely controlled explosion.'

'You've only given it a cursory glance, yet. Would you like to read more before we decide what to do with it, professor?' Walsh asked seriously.

'Oh yes. I would like to, and I think it would be wise.'

'Then do so, but please do your reading here in this Tudor wing. You've been more than just a great help to us, professor, you've been invaluable. I can't thank you enough. Reg, when you've sorted the dangerous papers from the innocuous ones, index them up and we'll classify them as top secret. You know what to do. I'll leave them in your charge.'

Reg Finch nodded seriously. 'No problem, but you do realise that Myres would have been able to read some of these papers, in the priest-hole? He would have known that a lot of them were about Hitler. Maybe that's why he put the body in the bunker, as a sick sort of joke.'

'He must have been mad, then. He should have left the body in the tunnel. If the professor hadn't turned up, the chances are it would never have been found,' Alison pointed out.

'But you don't know who else knew about the priest-hole, my dear,' the professor said quietly. 'Adrian's father told him about it, and he told Gregory. Perhaps Gregory told the next male in line to inherit. Presumably if he retained possession of this building it is still part of the original family entail.'

'Good Lord. Because the hotel was sold off I'd assumed that this wing was a disposable asset too, and that Mrs Fitzpatten would automatically get it,' Walsh admitted thoughtfully. 'We should have asked her that yesterday. There might be another heir. Would you have a word with her, Brenda? It may not be relevant, but we'd better know. Myres's mistake was to leave the catch in the locked position on the front door. He probably set it like that to make sure that no one could get in and disturb him while he disposed of the body, but he forgot to unlock it later. However, it still leaves two unanswered questions. If Myres is the killer, who bashed him on the head? And who set the National Front boys to break in and try for a bit of arson? Those two thugs are a bit of an enigma. I can't see how they fit in yet.'

'Maybe Myres organised the thugs, merely to cover any tracks he may have left,' Brenda suggested. 'In which case, since they were both caught in the act, perhaps one of their mates thinks that the whole thing was a set-up job to get two stooges to take the blame. Maybe he worked Myres over as a punishment.'

'That's a possibility,' Walsh mused. 'But I still can't see why Myres would need to hire anyone to set the place on fire, when he could easily have done it himself.'

'If Myres did arrange it with someone in London, he must have used the phone, boss, in which case the number he dialled may be recorded. I'll get in touch with the telephone company's liaison officer, and find out what calls he made,' Reg announced.

'Do that, then find out what you can about Myres. We need to find a motive if we're going to pin the murder on to him. Maybe he and Fitzpatten had a row about something. That'll keep you busy enough. Arthur, you can look into the Houghton assault. Reg thinks the wife and daughter might know what really happened. Go and see what you can make of it. Alison, you work on the missing Stilito. He was telling his woes to the Middlemarch woman, so talk to her, maybe he gave her a hint of where he might go.'

'I find it so fascinating, listening to you all planning this murder investigation,' the professor felt moved to say. 'There are so many different things going on. How on earth do you keep track of it all?'

'With great difficulty,' Walsh replied with a tired grin.

'Andy Myres?' Robin Sainsbury said in some surprise. 'Well, yes, I've known him for several years. We meet up occasionally, but I can't say I know him very well. He's a good instructor, and he's quite well thought of at the club here, I believe. He'll never be the life and soul of a party though, he's too withdrawn. Insular, I suppose you might say. He keeps himself to himself. Why do you ask? He's all right, isn't he?'

'Not at the moment he isn't. He's in hospital. He had an accident in his flat last night and hurt his head. I was just wondering – you sports instructors do have the reputation, rightly or wrongly, of sometimes getting involved with the women you give lessons to. Do you think there might be any jealous husbands around on his account?'

Robin Sainsbury reddened and looked sharply up at Reg Finch's enigmatic face. 'Good grief, I thought you lot were here investigating a murder. What the devil has poor old Andy's love life got to do with that?'

'I'm the one asking the questions. Have you heard any gossip about Myres being involved with any women, or any hint of anything unusual that might have happened recently? He wasn't married, so he didn't have to worry about a wife's feelings.'

Sainsbury frowned angrily and scratched his head. 'I wouldn't have thought he was involved with a woman. It never seemed to me that he got on very well with them, not socially, anyway. The only thing the remotest bit shady I've ever heard about him was when some of your lot found a couple of sets of second-hand clubs he was selling in his shop had been stolen. That can easily happen. When someone wants to buy a new set and part exchanges his old ones, you don't start asking too many questions about how he came by them, do you? But you'd know more about all that than I do. By the way, when can we start using the eighteenth green again?'

'When our forensic department are satisfied there's nothing more they can learn from it. I gather you want to do some nightmare therapy in the deep bunker. It's very good of you to give up so much of your time to help Amanda Knightly. That is her name, isn't it?'

'Yes, but it's the least I can do. She helped me win a good chunk of prize money, didn't she?'

Reg Finch shrugged his shoulders. 'That's true. It's none of my business, but you must have a very understanding wife too.'

'She was an understanding wife, and it is none of your business. She died two years ago, if you must know.'

Lynda Fitzpatten lounged in a sun chair in a corner of the hotel veranda. Beside her was a small table which still bore evidence of the unappetising weight-watcher's lunch that she had partly consumed – lettuce, tomatoes and cottage cheese. She was wearing less stylish, casual clothes today. Even so her mauve linen slacks and grey cotton shirt fitted her subtle curves to perfection, and the whole effect was still to ooze magnetic waves that drew men from near and afar to ogle her.

Detective Constable Brenda Phipps did not come into that category; she looked down with cool indifference at the face that had launched a thousand products. 'I'm sure you will be pleased to learn, Mrs Fitzpatten, that we've found the manuscript of the book your husband was writing. There was a secret cupboard in his study.'

'Oh, I *am* so pleased. I've been losing sleep over it,' Lynda Fitzpatten observed sarcastically.

'Have you now? It does show. Never mind. I have a couple of questions to ask. Firstly, are the Elizabethan wing and the hotel shares part of an entail, owned by a trust in perpetuity for whoever happens to be the head of the Fitzpatten family? If they are, then who is your late husband's heir in that respect?'

'They are entailed, but as to the heir, you'll have to ask his lawyers, Fiffe and Dottle, that question,' Mrs Fitzpatten replied sharply. 'His real heir is a ten-year-old bastard from his college days, paternity of whom was gleefully acknowledged as proof to the whole world that all his bits worked properly. Whether that one counts or not I don't know. The official Fitzpatten next-in-line is a cousin who lives in Hartlepool, of all places. What's the matter with you? Have you got a cold or something?' she went on, watching curiously as Brenda's nostrils twitched like a dog scenting the air.

'It's your perfume. Pretty strong stuff, isn't it? Distinctive too. You wore it the other day. Do you always use it?'

'It ought to be distinctive, it's one of the most expensive on the market. It's one of the few things I've advertised that I really like. It's called Lingering Passion. I use it all the time. It certainly does linger,' she said with a light laugh.

'Yes, it certainly does linger,' Brenda murmured absent-mindedly. Seemingly she was debating mentally what to say next, but that didn't take long. 'Tell me, Mrs Fitzpatten, why did you visit Andy Myres in his flat over the golf shop last night?' she asked bluntly.

Lynda Fitzpatten's eyebrows rose in shock and surprise at that unexpected question. Then her habit of making sharp clever ripostes led her to respond when it might have been wiser to have said nothing. 'Because he asked me to, of course,' she blurted out snappily.

'Did he now?' Brenda smiled triumphantly. Then she used her radio to summon assistance, in the form of Detective Chief Inspector Walsh.

Sidney Walsh looked anything but pleased. He'd been aimlessly whiling away half an hour before going up to the hospital to meet Gwen's consultant and learn the result of the biopsy. Now he was embroiled in a situation he couldn't ignore, and even a personal matter as important as that would have to give way to duty.

'We'd better go somewhere more private than this. Find out if we can use the manager's office, Brenda,' he suggested, looking at the bewildered and angry face of Lynda Fitzpatten. No doubt there would be some uncooperative bluster from her as she tried to retrieve her composure, and to blur or negate what she had admitted. The fact that she would not be able to achieve either would soon bring about a display of tears and contrived hysteria: a not uncommon occurrence when some women were faced with an unpleasant situation.

'What makes you think I was there?' Mrs Fitzpatten demanded aggressively, setting out a little late to discover just what the evidence against her was. Having entered the office first she had sat down at the hotel manager's desk and was leaning forward on her elbows glaring at the other two, as though it were she who was the interviewer and they the suspects.

'Did you wipe your fingerprints from all the door handles before you went out?' Walsh asked, raising his eyebrows interrogatively. That question caused Brenda's eyebrows to rise in sympathy too. As far as she was aware the scene of crime team had yet to make a report, and even if fingerprints had been found in the flat over the golf shop, it was a lengthy job to identify the salient features and make a positive identification. However, she could not help but admire the Chief's interviewing technique. His last question was doubly barbed; a simple Yes or No from Mrs Fitzpatten was still an admission that she had been there.

The woman's mouth hung limply open while her brain sought suitable unincriminating words.

'Well? Did you?' Walsh repeated, certain now that her prints would indeed be found within the golf shop. That certainty had also occurred to Mrs Fitzpatten, and the look on her face became that of a wild animal lured into an inescapable cage. Her bottom lip quivered indecisively as she shook her head, and looked away.

'The smell of your perfume was still in the room. Lingering Passion is quite unmistakable,' Brenda Phipps added in a voice that rang with the confidence of someone who had just put in place the final piece of a complicated jigsaw. Walsh looked dubious about the prospect of trying to present evidence of a smell to a future court of law, however to the woman at the desk it clearly seemed a more damning indictment than mere fingerprints.

'He's not dead yet, you know. You didn't kill him,' Walsh said consolingly. 'Why don't you just tell us what happened, before we hear his side of the story? He asked you to go and see him, did he?'

Lynda Fitzpatten decided once again that opposition was too painful, it was better to give in and let things run their course. Her other wiles might be advantageously brought into play later.

'He's not dead?' she said in surprise. 'He must have a really thick skull then. I hit him as hard as I could. Yes, he phoned me here in the hotel. He said he knew something vitally important,

129

and it was a matter of life or death that I go and see him. I never dreamt that with Gregory just dead, any man would be so callous as to pull a story like that, just to get me on my own. It shows how wrong you can be. I went to his place, and the dirty bugger tried to blackmail me. He said he would tell you lot that he saw me go in my own front door on the night Gregory was killed, unless I let him have sex with me. I was very frightened. He was all fired up, you see, and when men are like that, if you say no to them, they can get violent and hurt you. So I played along and let him do what he wanted, but only until I got hold of that golf club, then I didn't half give him a hell of a whack.'

'Why didn't you come to us? If he was attempting what you say, that's effectively rape, so you hit him in self-defence,' Brenda explained helpfully.

'I didn't want to get involved.'

'Myres could see your front path from his sitting-room window. Do you think he actually did see someone go to your front door that night, or was it just a story to get you on your own?'

She was thoughtful for a moment while she considered this. 'He was very convincing, and he said he'd moved Gregory's body out of the house so that there would be no direct evidence against me. Yes, he really did act as though he thought he'd got power over me, and that I'd be only too pleased to do whatever he wanted to keep him quiet. I was so shocked at the time I could hardly think straight. Yes, I do think he believed what he was saying. Maybe he did see someone go down my front path that night, but it wasn't me. I was in Nottingham. I've told you.'

'You certainly booked in at the hotel there, but it would have been very easy to have borrowed a car, come here, murdered your husband, and then driven back. There was plenty of time for that, and we do have a witness who says you were looking pretty tired next morning,' Walsh said accusingly.

'Oh my God, but I didn't. I didn't. Why don't you believe me?'

'Because this is a murder enquiry. We don't believe anything anybody says unless there's conclusive proof. Can you prove conclusively that it wasn't you who Myres saw?'

Lynda Fitzpatten looked reluctantly down at the backs of her slender hands. 'Yes, I can,' she said softly. 'If I have to.'

'Well, you jolly well do have to,' Brenda said aggressively. 'Did you spend the night your husband died sleeping with another man in that Nottingham hotel?'

There might have been another murder there and then, if looks were lethal, but Brenda survived it, then the look changed into one of pleading when it was transferred to Walsh's face.

'You will be discreet, won't you? I wasn't having a sordid affair, inspector. I don't do things like that. It was business. He's a married man, and I might lose his publicity contract if his wife found out. I know it's only a cheap skin care cream, but it could be worth a lot of money over the next two years. Surely you understand my position, inspector. No one lasts long in my business. I could easily be a has-been tomorrow if my luck runs out. I've just got to make money while the going is good,' she explained tearfully.

'Who was this man? What is his name?' Walsh demanded with a frown.

She could not bear to say the name out loud, presumably, so she used the hotel manager's pen to write it on a piece of paper, which she then folded and handed to Walsh.

'Funnily enough, I think I believe what she says,' Brenda Phipps announced with a curious look on her face that suggested she had surprised herself by finding anything remotely acceptable to say about Mrs Lynda Fitzpatten.

She may have surprised herself, but she surprised her two companions even more. Investigations into criminal activities did not have room for such expressions of faith in statements made during an interview, particularly when the individual concerned was on a short list of possible murderers.

'Believe? Believe what?' Walsh demanded, his face bearing a confused frown.

'That Myres genuinely thought he had seen her going into her house. Remember that Myres told Reg he thought Fitzpatten himself was away that evening, because his car wasn't there. Maybe Myres nipped down the secret passage hoping he'd see Lynda Fitzpatten undressing through Arthur's peepholes in the panelling. When he didn't, and the place was so quiet, he explored, and found Fitzpatten's dead body. Do you see? That must have convinced him even more that it was Mrs Fitzpatten he'd seen, and that may have been when the sex blackmail idea jumped into his head. For all he knew, if he left things as they were, Lynda Fitzpatten would be a prime suspect, and that wouldn't suit his new plan, so he shifted the body out to the bunker. Do you see what I mean? Myres is no fool. He would never have tried that blackmail trick if he hadn't been totally convinced that he would have real power over Mrs Fitzpatten.'

'But he was wrong, Brenda. He didn't have any power over Mrs Fitzpatten,' Reg pointed out.

'Precisely, Reg. That's just what I'm saying. Myres thought he'd seen Mrs Fitzpatten that night, but it wasn't her, so it must have been someone else.'

'You've made a good case, Brenda, but what does that mean? It's all surmise until we can question Myres himself,' Reg pointed out.

'That's true, Reg,' Walsh said thoughtfully, 'but when Myres comes out of his coma we may find he's changed his impressions about who he thought he saw. Maybe it's someone very like Mrs Fitzpatten in height and build, that he can put a different name to. She likes wearing slacks, so it could even have been a man he really saw. From our point of view it won't be proof, but it might well put us on the right path. We'll just have to wait and see.'

'But what if the news got around that Myres definitely saw someone going into the Elizabethan wing that night? Might not the murderer consider it a worthwhile risk to try and close Myres's memory down permanently?' Brenda suggested, a trifle light-heartedly.

'While we wait in ambush?' Reg added with a slight smile. 'It's a nice idea, but it wouldn't work. Myres is a sick man in Addenbrooke's Hospital. If the murderer knew that we knew that Myres might have seen him, then he'd know we'd have a guard on the ward, and we would have, of course. He wouldn't take the risk.'

'Yes, but what if we let out the story that Myres has regained consciousness, but won't be well enough for us to question him until tomorrow, yet he's well enough, because he hates hospitals, to discharge himself and come back here to his flat over his golf shop?' Walsh suggested, doggedly pursuing that line of thought and almost taking it seriously.

132

'That sounds pretty weak, Chief. I don't know if anyone would swallow a story like that.'

'They might do, if the story was being told by the right person,' Reg suggested positively. 'If Myres did want to come out of hospital he'd probably ring the green-keeper, Grant Finlay, and ask him to come and fetch him home. Honest as the day is long, is Finlay. If we got him on our side, and he told the story, it would be believed, and he's a chatterer too when he gets going, so that story would get all round the hotel and golf club, as well as the village. But Myres isn't going anywhere, unless we could replace him with a good look-alike actor.'

'And I know where to get one of those,' Brenda said with a broad mischievous grin. 'Arthur – Arthur Bryant. With a bandage round his head and a bit of make-up on his eyebrows, he'd do a treat, I think. He's much the same build. Provided someone didn't get too close, of course.'

'It wouldn't work. We'd need a much more plausible explanation than the truth for Myres's bang on the head, and anyway, how do we, the police, come to know that he saw someone the night Fitzpatten was killed, and why haven't we done something about it already?' Reg asked doubtfully.

'We'd say that Myres's bang on the head was an accident. That's the story he'll give out when he's up and about,' Walsh said thoughtfully. He couldn't really see where all this was leading, but the other two were certainly serious about it. 'As for your other point, the story could be that since Myres had told us that he couldn't put a name to the figure he'd seen, we'd arranged to collect together all the videos of the golf tournament and the ones of the guests leaving the hotel, so that he could sit and watch them at his leisure. Myres would be bound to spot the figure of the murderer, if he was on those videos, and then we could put a name to it.'

'Brilliant, I like that last bit, Chief. That really ought to get the murderer biting his fingernails worrying about what we do or don't know. A lot of the story is weak, but the knowledge that he had been seen, and might be recognised from the videos, ought to put him in a real panic. If he's still around. I think we should do it.'

'Do what?' Walsh demanded with a frown.

'Set up an ambush, of course,' Brenda responded impatiently. 'What do you think, Reg?'

'Yes, boss. I agree. We won't be any worse off if it doesn't work. Arthur can pretend to be a groggy Myres, and be seen to lock himself, alone, in the golf shop, but we can reinforce him through the secret tunnel. It's not brilliant, but it's better than nothing.'

Sidney Walsh looked down at his watch. He'd missed that appointment about the biopsy report with the consultant at the hospital, and the very thought of the word biopsy was sending waves of depression through his mind. In spite of the operation Gwen might have terminal cancer, and there would be nothing he could do about it, except watch her slowly die. Here he was, involved with this damned Fitzpatten case which was like a giant tangled ball of wool, with strands going off in all directions. Stilito, Houghton, and Myres, Mrs Fitzpatten, a shady Catholic priest, and any of dozens of hotel staff and guests, were pulling on those strands, laughing at him because his mind was too tired to be able to work out which one was a killer. It might take months to follow all those threads and while he was following them Gwen would be gradually dying. This hare-brained scheme to flush the killer from hiding sounded as nutty as anything he'd ever heard, but what the hell. His team seemed to think it was worthwhile, surely he could trust their judgement, and at least it was doing something, rather than just waiting, waiting for the end to come.

'Right then. We'll set it up, but there's not much time, so we might have to cut a few corners. We'll need to get the hospital management to co-operate with the Myres–Bryant switch. I'll get the CC involved with that. There's Arthur to sort out, and the green-keeper Finlay to get on our side. You'd better deal with that, Reg. Brenda, you'd better have a word with Mrs Fitzpatten, and tell her to keep her mouth shut about how Myres did get bashed on the head. We've got a lot to do, so I suggest we get on with it.'

10

'Sidney, as you get older your ambush plans get crazier and crazier,' the CC said grumpily, while rubbing the side of his big broad nose with a big broad finger.

'Well, maybe I'm getting wiser and wiser as I get older, too,' Walsh replied sharply.

'Don't get short-tempered with me, sunshine. If you've let your stress levels build up, it's your own fault. I told you to have some time off. Now, have you thought this ambush business through properly? It sounds a bit rushed,' the CC asked mildly.

'Yes, I think so. Mind you, I don't think our chances of success are very high, but if it were to come off, it would save us a tremendous amount of work. If it doesn't, we're no worse off, except for the loss of a night's sleep.'

'That's true. Do you want your team to be armed?'

Walsh nodded. 'The killer has a small-calibre pistol of some sort. It probably couldn't hit a barn door at ten paces, but there's no point in taking unnecessary chances. So, yes – light flak jackets and small arms.'

'Why do you want me to contact the hospital administration?'

'Because the hospital is even more hidebound with their paper-work and red tape than we are, so it would be best if this identity switch is set up at the highest level,' Walsh explained.

'All right. I'll set it up in principle with the registrar, but you'd better get over there to deal with the details. Before I do that, I want to talk to you about this business of a Catholic priest named Monserrat. I'm afraid I'm not doing all that well,' the CC admitted grimly. 'I know it sounds silly, but it seems almost as though the word has been put around in religious circles not to co-operate with any enquiries made by the Cambridgeshire Constabulary. That makes me think that something mighty fishy is going on. Still, I have managed to find some things out. There's a Monserrat in the Vatican's public relations area who has the reputation of being a "fixer" or trouble-shooter. Whether he's the one who saw Fitzpatten or not I don't yet know, but I have it on very good authority that the Vatican was aware that Fitzpatten had been making enquiries about that fellow Father Bernhard Stempfle who Hitler bumped off in the 1930s, and they weren't too happy about it either. Now, Scotland Yard has sent me a report saying that as far as they are concerned those two hired thugs are more likely linked to the Mafia than the National Front. So, do you know what I think? I think that this Monserrat fellow, when he failed to persuade Fitzpatten not to publish his book about Pope Pius XII, must have gone to the criminal underworld for help. Even Catholic thugs must go to Confession occasionally, and instead of a few "Hail Marys", I reckon a couple of them were told they'd have to earn their absolutions by going up to the Tudor wing, spraying "NF" all over the walls as a red herring, then setting out to destroy Fitzpatten's manuscripts and papers by putting a torch to the place when there was nobody about. I think that's highly likely, but it's going to be damned nigh on impossible to prove.' He shrugged his broad shoulders reluctantly, and drummed his fingers on his desk. 'Right, you want me to ring the hospital's registrar about this golf professional. What's his name again?'

Reg Finch found the elderly green-keeper, Grant Finlay, contentedly smoking his pipe and sitting in the afternoon sun on a sawn elm trunk; one that had been lopped of its branches and rolled to the back of the sixteenth tee, to be used, as it was being used, as a seat. He wore a floppy-brimmed grey felt hat to shade his face. His dog lay at his feet, wild-eyed and panting, its long pink tongue flicking up and down, and spraying out tiny drops of spittle which sparkled in the sunlight. Against the backdrop of trees and shrubs, the pastoral scene of man and dog might have been an enlargement of a detail from a Constable landscape.

'It's all right for some. Do you mind if I sit down too?' Reg asked pleasantly.

'Be my guest. I'm busy working, but you won't disturb me none,' Finlay replied. A slight twitch of his lips sufficed perhaps for a welcoming smile, while the cool grey eyes momentarily surveyed the face of the newcomer with all the shrewd precision and penetration of an X-ray machine.

'Problems to ponder?' Reg enquired pleasantly, seating himself down on the elm trunk, which had been finely polished over the years by countless backsides.

'Yes. You see that big tree down the fairway there, on the corner, where the dog-leg goes to the right. That's a Douglas Fir, that is. It's about a hundred and thirty, nigh on a hundred and forty feet high just now, and it's still growing. He could go on for another thirty or forty feet yet, if not more. There's one in Wales that's over a hundred and eighty feet, so they tell me. Well, he's my problem,' Finlay explained.

'I like trees,' Reg said, 'and that one's a beauty. You ought to be proud of it.'

'Oh I am, and so are plenty of others, but there's them as don't like it at all, at least, not where it is. Lengthwise this sixteenth is a longish par four, you see. That dog-leg's nigh on three hundred yards from the tee, further than your average golfer can drive, but it didn't use to matter much, because with a six or seven iron they could put their second shots high over the corner, and they'd end up on the green, five times out of ten. But that tree's got so big now they can't cut the corner off, because they can't get up and over it. So they has to chip up to the bend of the dog-leg and go round it that way, but that costs them an extra stroke, and that's what they don't like. The committee's been told to do something about it, and there's even been talk of felling it. "Like hell," I told them. "I'm not cutting down a tree like that just to knock a stroke off a bloody score card." So they said that if I felt that way about it, I'd have to come up with a better solution. Typical, isn't it? That's what they call delegating authority, these days. It used to be called passing the bloody buck. Anyway, never mind. Sitting here thinking, quiet like, I reckon I've come up with an answer.'

'You have? Well done,' Reg said with a smile.

'Aye! If we can make this hole twenty yards longer, it'll be long enough to be a par five. That'd give them their extra stroke for the dog-leg, and then they'll be happy.'

'How do you make the hole longer?' Reg asked with interest.

'Make this the ladies' tee and lay out another men's tee, twenty yards back there. That's no problem. There's only a few scrubby young birch and brambles would have to go. So that's my problem dealt with. Now what about yours? You didn't come all the way out here to find me, just to pass the time of day, now did you?'

'True, very true,' Reg acknowledged, pulling at his jaw thoughtfully. 'We wondered if you'd help us set up a little undercover operation. Highly secret and confidential, of course.'

The grey eyes that stared at Reg's face showed a flicker of interest. 'You'll be wanting to set a trap for young Gregory's killer, I suppose. Well, I've done a bit of that sort of thing myself, in Malaya, years ago. We'd stake out a trail to a village in the jungle that we knew the terrorists were using. Then me and me mates would lay out there, dead silent, for days and nights on end, not moving a muscle, until the bastards came creeping along. Then we'd shoot the bloody lot quick, before they could shoot us. But your killer won't make a move unless he has to, so what kind of bait can you dangle that's strong enough to tempt him to risk his neck by coming out into the open?'

'Are you going to help us, or not? I'll need your promise of absolute secrecy. That's vital,' Reg insisted.

'Too right it is. If anyone had blabbed about the traps we set in the jungle, it would have been us that got shot up, not them. I can keep my mouth shut. Yes, I'll help you if I can,' Finlay said with an earnestness at variance with his usual casual attitude.

'Right! I'll tell you what we have in mind. Andy Myres is the bait. He's in hospital at the moment, because he had an accident last night, and banged his head. However, we want it put about that he's told us that he saw someone go into Fitzpatten's place, the night of the murder, and tomorrow he's going to be watching all the videos of the golf tournament, and those we've got of the hotel guests and staff coming and going, together with a few we've put together of the people in the village. It'd be surprising if the killer's not on them somewhere, for Myres to spot,' Reg explained.

'That's the story, is it? Well, it won't wash. It just don't sound right.'

'I haven't finished yet.'

'Hold hard. Let me get to grips with what you've just said. How come Andy had an accident last night, and banged his head?'

'That doesn't matter. It was an accident. He had a fall and cracked his head.'

'Oh aye. So it just happened, did it? When did Andy tell you he'd seen someone, then?'

'Late last night. When he looked out of his lounge window it made him remember he'd done the same thing the night before. That's when he realised he might have seen the killer. He phoned us right away, but it was too late to do anything then, you see.'

'That's about as weak as the other bit, but go on. Did Andy really see someone, or is that just a story?'

'It's no story.'

'Right. So why can't Andy see your videos this afternoon, or this evening?'

'He's badly concussed and the doctors won't let us question him today. Tomorrow is the earliest we can do that.'

Finlay's face screwed up in an exaggerated expression of pain. 'You don't need an ambush and a load of judges to get justice done, mate. Gregory's killer is going to curl up and die laughing when he hears this lot. You really can't seriously expect anyone to try and get at Andy while he's in hospital? Oh, I know you read of people who put on a white coat, hang a stethoscope round their neck and wander about in them hospitals as much as they please, but I don't reckon it's quite as simple as that – besides, it's obvious that you'll have one of your men keeping an eye on him, since he's such an important witness. I don't know now if I can help you after all. A story like that just won't be believed.'

To Finlay's surprise Reg Finch was nodding his agreement. 'Absolutely right. Let me finish telling you the plan. You're right about hospitals but that doesn't apply, because Andy Myres hates being in that sort of place, and is going to discharge himself, against medical and police advice, of course.'

'He is, is he?'

'Yes, and guess who he's going to ring up and ask to come and collect him from the hospital, and bring him back here?'

'I think I get the picture. That's where I come in, I suppose.'

'Right, and since it'll be him telling you his story while he's in your car, it won't be rumour and gossip, but straight from the horse's mouth. Your mouth,' Reg explained with a grin.

'That's more like it,' Finlay acknowledged, reaching down absent-mindedly to tweak his dog's ears. 'That might work, particularly as Andy can tell it all himself. He can spread the word around in the hotel, while I do the village.'

'Not exactly,' Reg murmured. 'The Andy Myres you pick up from the hospital will be one of our officers made up to look like him. The real Andy Myres is being operated on to relieve a build-up of pressure within his skull. He won't be going anywhere for a while. The spreading of the story will be all down to you. You'll call in the local shop to get some milk, bread and coffee, then take the Andy look-a-like straight to his golf shop, where he'll go in, lock the door, and take himself off to bed, because for all his bravado, he's not feeling very well.'

'So you stake out the golf shop for the rest of the evening and night, waiting for a killer to come along?'

'You don't need to worry about that. That's our problem. All we want you to do is to tell the story as widely as you can without giving the impression that you're spreading it deliberately. Now, will you do it? We need to get things set up. There's not much time.'

'I must be mad, but yes, I'll do it.'

'Whose bright idea was it that I should get this job?' Arthur Bryant protested in a hushed voice. He was sitting on a chair in a small room off the corridor leading to the intensive care facilities of Addenbrooke's Hospital.

'Mine,' Brenda Phipps announced cheerfully, turning to select a different oily-wax crayon from the actor's make-up box which lay open on the nearby table.

'I think I ought to have been asked first,' Arthur grumbled, fingering the tight wad of bandages that circled his head. 'How did you know I would be prepared to take on a dangerous job like this? I might have had a date with a girl tonight or something.'

'Of course we knew you'd do it. It's well known that whenever there's a difficult and dangerous assignment that sets the knees of our bravest warriors trembling with fear, then there's only one real man for the job, and that's – Arthur Bryant. Already his fame has spread far and wide throughout the known world. In the African bush they have a Swahili name for him that loosely translated means "he who fears not to tread where no man's boot has gone before". Which is another way of saying "he who is always sticking his big foot in it". The word to our Anglo-Saxon ears sounds something like "Muddlehead".'

Arthur's eyebrows came together in a frown.

'That's just perfect, Arthur. Keep it like that. That's spot on. Even Andy Myres's mother wouldn't notice the difference.'

'How on earth am I supposed to prepare myself to act out this rotten part when you keep winding me up, Brenda?' Arthur mumbled sulkily, staring forward into the mirror at his transformed face and the devilish dark eyebrows that Brenda Phipps had so painstakingly been constructing.

'The more your spring's wound up the longer you'll keep ticking,' Brenda said, smiling encouragingly.

'I'm not a clock, and I wouldn't want to keep ticking if I'd got to live with a face like this for the rest of my life. Haven't you finished yet?'

'I've just got to do some bags under your eyes and to whiten the skin of your face. You've got to look pale, and even more sickly than you usually do.'

Arthur had no chance to riposte to that, since the door opened and Sidney Walsh came in.

'That's fine, Arthur. You're just about ready, I think,' Walsh said approvingly, as he sat himself down on a chair. 'The paperwork has all been sorted out. Officially you are now Andy Myres, and against strenuous medical advice, you've discharged yourself from the hospital. I did the voice-over bit for you, and I've rung the hotel to ask Finlay to come and fetch you. He's got a clear head on him, that old boy – he went straight off to ask if he could borrow Houghton's car. So the story is already starting to get around. Let's just run through your part again. You walk slowly and steadily down to the front entrance. Don't over-act the grogginess, otherwise you might have some stray doctors or nurses wanting to whisk you back into Casualty, and that would complicate things. When you meet Finlay down there, act as Myres would act. Tell him whereabouts you hit your head, but do it slowly. Remember, you've a hell of a headache, and you're feeling pretty low. On the way to the hotel Finlay will stop at the village shop to get you some milk, bread and coffee, and set the gossip going there. You don't get out of the car, of course. At the golf shop, go in, bolt the front door behind you, and go upstairs and get into bed. Don't move about, or don't be seen to move about in front of the windows. We'll wait until it's dark before reinforcements come in through the secret passage. The downstairs shop is far too open an area, so we won't keep changing minders. Brenda and Reg will stay upstairs with you for the rest of the night. Just remember your training, and stay alert. Right, time for you to go, I think, Arthur. Good luck.'

'Bloody hell. You don't half look like Andy,' Grant Finlay exclaimed, when they were both in Houghton's car and heading towards Trumpington. 'Back there in the hospital I really thought you were him. Close up I knows you're not, but you're damned good all the same. You've done a fair bit of acting before, I reckon.'

'Not a lot,' Arthur admitted modestly. 'We did *Macbeth* at school. I was one of the witches doing "Bubble, bubble, toil and trouble" and all that. You never know what you're going to be doing next, in my line of work.'

'I can see that. Bait, that's what you are. In India, when they're after a tiger, they stake out a goat in a clearing. Then they get up a tree with their rifles and wait until the poor old tiger gets hungry. There's never a thought for what happens to the old goat, he's expendable,' Finlay explained.

'It's not quite the same in my case, I hope, and I'm no helpless goat,' Arthur pointed out.

'That's true, and you won't be on your own likely, when someone comes in to try and kill you tonight. How are your minders going to get in without being seen? I know that place, and it ain't going to be easy. There's people about nearly all the time, golfers, guests, hotel staff and so on. You can't be sure if anyone's watching or not.'

Arthur resisted the temptation to tell about the secret passage. That was something Finlay didn't need to know about, but he sought for an answer to give anyway. 'There won't be any coming and going once I get in. The others will already be there. Yes,

142

you're right, it's not an easy place to stake out, so rather than risk spooking the person we're after, we're not going to stake it out. The killer will have free passage. She'll be tempted to come right up to the bait, and it'll be up to me to spring the trap, when I'm good and ready.'

'She? You think it's a woman? Have you got anyone in mind?' Finlay asked, turning his head sharply to glance at his passenger's face.

'Maybe. Most murders turn out to be crimes of passion, and Fitzpatten was a womaniser. I know women. If they get all serious about a man like that, particularly the young girls, they want him all to themselves, and they get awfully jealous when he goes after someone else,' Arthur explained earnestly.

'That's true enough. Lucy Stilito is a young girl, but I can't see her killing young Gregory, because she liked him too much,' Finlay murmured.

'True, but she's one of the soft easy ones. She'd swallow any kind of line, but you take someone like Houghton's eldest girl who I was talking to earlier today. I can't see Fitzpatten not giving her a dose of charm, even if she is no peach, but she's as hard as nails. If Fitzpatten played fast and loose with her, I can see her shoving the knife in him, can't you?'

'I hope not. I'm her godfather, and I promised in church to protect her and keep her free from sin,' Finlay muttered coldly. 'Here's the village shop. You hang on a minute while I go in and get the stuff you want. I won't be long.'

'Get some chocolate bars as well, will you? I'm going to need something more than bread to keep the wolf from the door during the night. I'm starving already,' Arthur exclaimed, rubbing his supposedly empty stomach.

'If you're going to be the bait, you should want the wolf to come to your door, but I'll see what I can get.'

Having delivered the pseudo Andy Myres to the now repaired front door of the golf shop, Grant Finlay reversed the hotel manager's car back up the narrow track to the car-park. The first person he met as he went to return Houghton's car keys was the winning professional of the recent golf tournament, Robin Sainsbury.

'They say you've been to see Andy at the hospital. How is he? Is he going to be all right?' Robin Sainsbury asked anxiously.

'Oh aye. He'll be as right as rain tomorrow, more than like. It were a silly thing to bang his head like he did, but there weren't nothing broken. The hospital wanted to keep him in for observation, but he weren't having none of that. He wanted out, so I've just dropped him off at his place. He's gone to bed with a dose of sleeping pills.'

'Is it true what they're saying, that he saw someone go into the murdered man's house, the night he was killed?' Robin asked.

'So he says. He don't know who it was, though. Familiar, he says, but he can't give a name to them just yet. He reckons he will tomorrow, when he sees all the police videos.'

'I'm surprised the police have let him come home on his own.'

'Why? He's a free man, ain't he? They can't stop him doing what he wants to do, besides, they'll be keeping an eye on him, no doubt. They had a patrol car coming round every hour and a half, regular as clockwork, last night, checking on Fitzpatten's place. I saw them. Like as not they'll do the same again tonight, for the golf shop,' Finlay pronounced confidently.

This spreading of the story, Finlay found out, was not going to be as difficult as he had originally thought. People actually came to seek him out, and they brought up the subject of Andy Myres and who he might or might not have seen on the night Gregory Fitzpatten was killed. He didn't have to actually spread the rumours, they had already spread, all he needed to do was give them substance, with a few confirmatory words delivered in his own inimitable dead-pan style. It was hardly surprising that so much unaccustomed talking should give him a dry throat, and to alleviate that he obtained a quart glass of bitter from the bar, and made his way carefully round the eighteenth green, to a seat in the old stone summerhouse. There, free from unwanted company for a little while, he could light his pipe, and relax, and watch the lithe young woman who had won the Wedgwood dinner service practise with her sand iron at the almost impossible task of getting a ball placed near the steep front face up and out of the Man Trap bunker. Clearly she had overcome any fear of uncovering another dead body, but it was quite obvious that she was now suffering the usual golfer's frustration with deep steep-sided bunkers. Her face had reddened with the effort, and after at least a dozen attempts, she had still to get the ball to rise nearly vertically in a shower of sand and lop up on to the green. Sainsbury could do it. He'd shown her twice already. He was a fine golfer, with a nice smooth swing. He ought to have done better for himself than becoming a mere club professional giving lessons and selling gear for a living, Finlay mused to himself, but what was happening in the bunker was a distraction to his thoughts. His mind had set itself to relive the day's unusual events and ponder on the trap that he had helped the police to set up. They were a cool lot, those of the police team that he'd met. They appeared to know just what they were about, and that gave one the impression that they knew far more about young Gregory's death than they were letting on – but would the murderer actually be tempted to break into the golf shop and venture upstairs, where the trap was waiting to be sprung?

The memories of the ambushes he had been involved in, in the Pahang jungle of far away Malaya came back into his mind as fresh as they ever had been. They had been risky ventures. Any involuntary move from either of his mates might have given their positions away, then the hunters would have become the hunted. That might happen tonight. Did they accept the risks, as he had had to do all those years ago? A sudden stirring of his brain told him that he must be out there tonight, to see it for himself. He knew these woods and shrubberies nearly as well as he knew the back of his hand – surely there was somewhere where he could be perfectly concealed, and yet still be able to see what was going on . . .

Having seen Arthur set off on his adventures, Sidney Walsh went down to the hospital's reception area, to buy some flowers, before going back up to visit Gwen.

The bed in the small room off the main ward, however, was ruffled but empty.

Surprise led to near panic as the worst scenario thoughts of critical relapses, heart attacks or a dozen other lethal maladies presented themselves in awful illogical sequence to his brain.

His breathlessly staccato demand of, 'What's happened? Where is she?' made to the first nurse he could find, merely elicited an amazed look at the distraught face of her abrupt questioner, and the offhand comment that his wife was probably in the communal sitting-room at the far end of the ward.

And there she was, sitting by the window, in the rainbow-coloured Chinese silk dressing-gown he'd bought for her last year. Pink-cheeked and bright-eyed, she was chattering away enthusiastically to a fair-haired bespectacled woman who was sitting beside her.

'This is my husband,' Gwen announced proudly, smiling up at him radiantly.

'I'm pleased to meet you,' Walsh said, rapidly switching from utter confused despair to the first available sociability mode in his brain's list of behaviour programs.

'Sidney, did you know that Christina's younger sister went to the same college as I did? Isn't that a coincidence?' Gwen went on chirpily.

'Amazing,' Walsh responded dutifully. 'I must say you're looking a whole lot better than you did yesterday, dear.'

'I feel it too. This morning the consultant told me that everything is fine. I'll be able to come home in a day or two.'

'Did he mention the biopsy?' Walsh asked, trying to keep the grating tone of anxiety from his voice.

'Oh yes, but that's fine too. There's absolutely nothing at all to worry about.' Sidney really did look handsome when he smiled as though he hadn't care in the world. What a pity he didn't smile like that a bit more often.

Reg Finch followed Brenda Phipps down the steps into the now not so secret tunnel. This he was not looking forward to. He and his lanky six foot one frame liked fresh air and open spaces, not dank and gloomy confined passages, barely a yard wide and four feet high. As he had expected, the roof was too low for him to be able to walk with his body merely bent forward, so he had to bend his knees into a crouch. Progress then became an undignified waddle that was extremely stressful on his leg and thigh muscles. He couldn't keep that up for long, so there was no alternative but to change to a hands and knees crawl, and in no time he felt absolutely filthy. He could not avoid the hanging dead roots that brushed his hair, or the foul slimy places on the floor, or the odd desiccated corpses of mice and rats. Brenda suffered from no such problems. Soon she was far ahead and she had to wait impatiently where the tunnel branched, for her longer limbed colleague to catch up.

'Oh, do come on, Reg,' she whispered irritably. 'What are you doing? Studying each and every stone or something? Forget the damned history, we've got work to do.'

Reg wisely ignored those comments, but unwisely brushed his hair from his forehead with a filthy hand.

'Down there, is it?' he said bluntly. 'You go on. I'll get there in my own good time.'

So Brenda went on alone. Dirt, dead rats and spiders did not bother her, at least, not when there was someone within call. She came to the trap door, switched off her torch, then slowly and carefully pushed it open. The hinges had been oiled only that afternoon, so it made no sound, and neither did she as she reached up to open the small door in the cupboard under the stairs. Then she climbed out into the golf shop. It was surprisingly bright in there. The moonlight was streaming through the windows that faced the path. Any watcher would see her if she stayed standing, so she dropped to her hands and knees, and stuck her head back in the tunnel.

'Turn your torch off, Reg,' she whispered. 'It's nearly as bright as day up here.'

There was a mumbled reply, but she could not make out what it was, so she scampered off round to the stairs and went up. The fifth wooden stair tread creaked loudly, but beyond that was the darkness of shadow where she could stand upright and creep properly. No doubt Arthur would have heard that stair creak, and would realise that his minders had arrived, but she would need to take great care now. Arthur might just think that noise had been made by Fitzpatten's killer creeping up to kill him, and be nervously alert as a result, ready to pounce on whoever came in.

The bedroom door was slightly ajar. Cautiously she pushed it open wider, and at the same time whispered loudly, 'It's all right, Arthur, it's only me – Brenda.'

There was no reply at all as she stepped into the room.

In the dimness she could see a dark figure lying on its side on the bed. It was prone and apparently lifeless. Her heart may have leapt figuratively into her mouth, but it was real fear that dried her throat and set her swallowing anxiously. Had the killer pre-empted their plans and arrived here before them? Had the life of Arthur, the Myres look-alike, and her colleague in arms, already been taken? That would be an utter disaster. She might tease him because of his youth and naïveté, but if he were now dead he would be sorely and tearfully missed.

She hurried over to the bed. In the gloom she could see no obvious signs of death. There was no knife in his back or pool of spreading blood on the sheets.

'Arthur! Arthur!' she whispered, as she shook his shoulder anxiously.

'Eh! What? What?' Arthur said loudly, instinctively jerking himself up on one elbow.

Brenda's dread turned to icy anger.

'For God's sake, Arthur, you are a stupid idiot. You were fast asleep. I could have crept up and slit your throat a dozen times over, and you would never have known. A fat lot of good you are on a mission like this.'

'For heaven's sake calm down, Brenda,' Reg whispered authoritatively as he too came in. 'It doesn't matter, there's no harm done. Let's get ourselves sorted out. I'll be in the sitting-room. Brenda, you make yourself comfortable behind the door in here. Arthur, if you go to sleep again I'll personally wring your scraggy neck. Right, no more talking. Keep your ears pinned back and stay alert.'

Silence reigned in the apartment over the golf shop, except for occasional soft creaks and groans as the ancient timbers adjusted to the expansion stresses and strains of temperature changes, plus a few natural noises from outside; the hoots of owls, for instance, and the faint wind stirring and rustling the leaves on the trees.

Now the trap was well and truly set, and there was nothing else to do but wait and see if anyone would come to spring it.

148

11

The mild May night was passing steadily by with its usual peaceful, patient inevitability. Well, peaceful for some. There were those nocturnal creatures praying, no doubt, that they could do unto others what they hoped would not be done unto themselves. For those doomed to die, and those about to dine, the night was a time of vigilance and fear, and sudden violence.

The vigilance of those human watchers in the vicinity of the golf shop was difficult to maintain. This was an unnatural extension of a day that had already been full and active, and tiredness was bound to dull the senses. Circumstances prevented the operation of alternating watches when each might have rested by turn, for any movement in this shrubby environment would be easily seen and far too risky.

So, Alison Knott, sitting well back from the upper bedroom window of the Tudor wing where she could observe the path approach to the front of the golf shop, struggled to keep herself merely awake, let alone bright and alert.

Sidney Walsh, with a characteristic refusal to accept the soft option to which his rank and age would surely have entitled him, had decided that a rhododendron deep in the scrubby growth on the other side of the path would give him the opportunity to watch the path from the car-park side, as well as one of the approaches to the back and near side of the ancient building that was now a golf shop. Earlier he had taken over half an hour to travel the hundred yards or so to this observation post, by sinuously crawling on his elbows and his belly. The task had given him a youthful sense of achievement, but, now that he lay secure beneath the verdant foliage, the need for continuous observation from a prone position was causing him problems. Keeping his head raised in order to peer forward very soon had the muscles in the back of his neck protesting. Moving cautiously into a sitting position eased that problem, but meant that his view was obscured by the shrub's lower branches. The compromise of lying on his side was far from ideal, but his eyes could stare out into the gloomy stillness confident that his brain would react to the slightest sign of movement.

In the meantime his thoughts set out to review recent events. The most significant of those, of course, was finding Gwen suddenly restored to something like her normal self, and learning that the biopsy report contained only good news. The feeling of relief as his fears and tension had evaporated away had been an incredible experience. Now the future was bright and positive again, not dark and depressing.

After that his mind settled into a methodical routine and proceeded to review the progress of the investigation into the case of Gregory Fitzpatten, deceased. Real evidence was sparse, not an uncommon feature in murder cases, unfortunately: merely a few splinters of thin glass that might have come from a small picture or photograph frame, and a small Italian coin which might have been loose change from the pocket of the deceased, his wife or a Catholic priest from Rome, or a token used to mark the place of a golf ball on a putting green. Were the two thugs who had purported to be National Front activists really hired as arsonists by a Catholic priest, in an attempt to destroy the manuscript of a book which would seriously embarrass the Church authorities in the Vatican if it were published? It was beginning to look the most likely explanation. If Reg and Brenda had not turned up at the Tudor wing when they had, the thugs might have succeeded too. With so much dry old timber in the place, once flames had taken a hold it would soon have ended up as just a pile of ashes, and the political and racial secrets of the past would have remained secret for ever. If that were true at least the Church had not involved itself in the sin of murder. Others certainly had committed sins of a lesser kind – a blackmailer's demand for sex, a wife's businesslike infidelity, and the deceased's many affairs and taste for the innocence of young girls. The motive for the murder might be political, or simply one of love, hate or revenge. Money seemed to play no obvious part. His mind set out to try and examine the basic characters of the individuals being closely or loosely investigated. That was more promising, for there were some interesting inconsistencies in and among them. They were probably simple coincidences, but on the other hand, with a little bit of speculation and a lot of imagination, they could be developed into an acceptable motive – for a mind as sick as a murderer's must be.

On the other side of the golf shop it was not duty that made Grant Finlay forsake his comfortable bed, but simple curiosity, and a desire to relive the adventures of his military youth. The corrugated iron shed that housed the golf course's lawn-mowers and other equipment made a suitable hiding place for someone to watch from, provided that someone had had the foresight to earlier bend out a few inches of corrugated sheet in one corner, to make a viewing slot.

Upstairs in the timber-framed building there was total silence as three pairs of sensitive ears tuned themselves to catch the slightest alien sound.

At ten minutes past one o'clock, a uniformed, torch-waving, cigarette-smoking police officer strolled casually down the path, walked round the building checking the doors and windows, then walked unhurriedly back to his patrol car, which was then heard to drive away.

That visit perked up the senses of all the watchers and listeners for a short time, but then the isolation and disorientation, where minutes seemed hours, and hours seemed minutes, and strained eyes actually seemed to see whole bushes and shrubs move, reasserted a sort of mental status quo.

It was at half past one that the black-garbed figure first appeared, flitting through the bushes that fringed the car-park, although there was no one stationed there to see it. It made its way silently from shrub to shrub through the undergrowth that bordered the path, heading towards the rear of the golf shop.

Sidney Walsh was the first to see its fleeting movement, but that was out of the corner of one eye, so his partly numbed mind needed to replay the scene again before he comprehended its apparent reality. The report he breathed slurringly into the microphone of his radio was terse – too terse.

151

'I see a prowler,' he mumbled softly.

Most of those who were equipped to hear him maintained a stony silence. It was Alison who responded coldly: 'Going where, sir?'

Walsh was already on his hands and knees, crawling cautiously towards the rear of the building.

'It's going towards the back of the building. It's out of sight now,' he replied blandly.

To him it was, but Finlay could now see it. A shadow that was darker than the darkness, moving at the rear of the shop. It appeared to bend down and place something on the ground, then seemed to be fumbling at one of the leaded windows. Finlay's vision switched on some adrenalin-induced light enhancement facility. A knife or chisel was being used to prise away the soft lead strip from around one small pane of glass until it could be eased away from the rest. A hand reached in through the space to release the catch, and then the window was opened. The figure with its bundle climbed through, and was then out of sight. With his heart beating faster, Finlay realised that he hadn't thought things through properly. What was he now to do? Remain inactive and merely observe? Or do something positive? The issue wasn't really in doubt. The intruder went in through the window, and would therefore come out through the window. If he, Finlay, was waiting outside, he would make the vital capture. He moved stealthily to take up that position. By hook or by crook, he was going to be in at the kill, if he could.

Inside the building, the figure paused to plan a way through the assorted golf trolleys and racks of clubs, then stepped warily and silently towards the front door. The catch of the Yale lock was eased back, and with the faintest of clicks, was locked into the open position. There was also a single bolt, and that too was silently drawn. That allowed another means of escape other than the window. So far, things had gone very well. No noise had been made at all, and there was no sign of anyone lying in wait. So, dealing with a man effectively anaesthetised by sleeping pills was going to be easier than it first appeared.

The figure crept over to the stairs and removed the caps from both of the petrol-filled plastic two-litre lemonade bottles that had been such a burden to carry. One was stood, still full, on the fifth wooden stair. That would provide an explosive bomb effect. The contents of the other were poured liberally over the dry wooden staircase and a nearby rack full of waterproof coats, keeping enough to run a thin line of the inflammable liquid over the stone floor to the front door. That would be the fuse. The figure opened the front door wide, a good draught would soon be needed. A cigarette lighter set flame to a hastily twisted golf club price list, and that, dropped on the fuse, ignited it – with the dangerously explosive *whoosh* that takes all those who light fires with petrol by surprise.

The figure turned and ran out through the doorway.

The job was done, but the need for as much care and caution in the escape as had been taken in the approach was swamped by panic. There was just a terrible need to get as far away from that awful blazing inferno as one could, and in the shortest possible time.

The blinding flash of flame took all the watchers by surprise.

For Walsh, it meant a heart-stopping moment of fear for the safety of those of his team upstairs within the building, but a quick upwards glance at the undamaged windows of the apartment reassured him that the fire was not yet in those rooms, so the three within should have no problem in exiting safely, and would no doubt be doing so at any moment. Then the new source of light revealed the crouching form of Grant Finlay by the open rear window, waiting for the intruder to leave, but to Walsh it was as if that unknown person had just leaped from the window, and it was not unreasonable for him to assume it was Fitzpatten's killer, now having added arson to his list of crimes. Walsh charged at the unsuspecting Finlay, with thoughts and feelings that contained little kindness or consideration.

Finlay did not remain unsuspecting for long. He caught a glimpse of Walsh's obviously hostile approach out of the corner of his eye and, with reactions remarkable in a man of his years, was off like a shot, attaining a zero to sixty ratio of acceleration that many cars would be envious of. He scampered off round the back of the building, across the path, and went crashing and blundering through the dark shrubs and undergrowth, out on to the eerie moonlit open area of the eighteenth green, with Walsh pounding along in hot pursuit.

Alison Knott, however, in accordance with the prearranged plan of action once a suspect intruder had been sighted, had abandoned her surveillance position in the Tudor wing bedroom, and hurried down the stairs and out to the path. There she crept cautiously towards the golf shop. She saw the front door being opened, and a few seconds later the blinding flash of the igniting petrol within. She was so close when the dark figure came dashing out of the blazing building that she was only a few yards away from making a dramatic capture, but by the time she had turned to follow, and built up speed, she was already many yards behind and losing ground. Undaunted, she pressed on with the intention of keeping her quarry in sight. It was something of a shock when two further figures sped out of the darkness to her left. She ignored them, even when the second of the two made a diving tackle and brought the one in front crashing to the ground, because she had troubles of her own. From the gloom ahead, where her quarry had just gone, another dark shape had materialised; it was clearly moving to intercept her and cut her off from her quarry. There was little she could do except veer away to her right, try to put on more speed, and at the last moment swerve sideways to avoid contact, but it was all to no avail. The dark figure's dive brought outstretched arms grasping round her thighs, and she, too, was brought thudding to the ground. Anger and fear made her react quickly. She brought her open right hand round in a swinging chopping blow that landed with a painful thud on the side of her assailant's head. That effected her release from the grasping arms and, as she leapt to her feet, she swung one of them hard into her assailant's stomach. That eliminated all signs of aggression from that quarter. When she looked round there was no sign of her original quarry.

The two characters behind her were engaged in a rolling swearing wrestling match, but one voice she recognised, so she went over to restore law and order there. She bent to grab an appropriate arm and twisted it up behind an appropriate back, then calmly informed Sidney Walsh that he could leave go now.

154

That gave Grant Finlay the opportunity to gasp out, 'For crying out loud, I'm on your side, ain't I? Get off me, you hulking great elephant. I reckon you've busted me ribs – and me neck and all, I shouldn't wonder.'

'Hello, Mr Finlay,' Alison observed coolly and politely. 'Are you all right?'

'No, I'm not. I'm bashed and bruised all over.'

Walsh had got to his feet now. 'Well, what the devil were you doing back there?'

'The same as you, I reckon. I set the damned trap up for you, you surely didn't expect me to go away all meek and mild and have nothing more to do with it, did you?' He was still hoarse and panting for breath. 'I was watching from my equipment shed, and I saw the beggar go in through the blasted window. I was waiting for him to come out the same way, when you started chasing me.'

'Whoever it was went out of the front door. I just missed him, and I was chasing, until that one came charging out of the bunker, and knocked me over,' Alison informed them, having released her hold on Finlay's arm.

'Who the hell is that?' Walsh demanded.

'I don't know, yet,' Alison admitted.

The figure was struggling to its feet as the three of them went over.

'That's Sainsbury, the golfer,' Finlay prompted softly.

'Well, Mr Sainsbury,' Walsh said sternly. 'And what are you doing out here tonight, and why the hell did you attack one of my officers?'

Sainsbury tried to straighten up, but the effort obviously hurt since he grunted in pain and so he remained bent forward, with one hand held tightly to his stomach.

'How the hell was I supposed to know who it was?' he gasped. 'I reckoned someone might have a go at Andy Myres tonight, so I've been in the woods here, keeping an eye open for trouble. When I saw the flash of the bomb going off, and then this officer of yours came running, I assumed she'd done it. I was only trying to help. What about Andy? Is he all right? Did he get out all right?'

'I should imagine so.' Walsh stared at him and shook his head thoughtfully. 'It really is nice to find that the public are all so

155

fired ready to help the police in their fight against crime. But I'm afraid the old adage still holds good. Too many cooks do spoil the broth.' He turned away. 'Come on, Alison. Let's go and see if the others are all right, and we'd better make sure the fire brigade's been alerted.'

The three in the rooms above the golf shop were not all right.

No sounds had drifted up from below even to inform them that an intruder was inside, let alone to indicate what that person might be getting up to. The smell of petrol had not wafted upstairs either, even though the invisible fumes had filled the stair well. So the police team were taken completely by surprise at the sudden blowtorch-like blast of flame on the small landing.

Brenda Phipps, sitting on a stool and leaning forward with her elbow resting on her knee and her chin on her hand, was behind the half-open bedroom door. The blast flung that door wide open, hitting her a numbing blow on the head, and knocking her sideways to the floor.

Arthur Bryant leapt off the bed and stared aghast at the giant tongues of flame flicking in through the doorway and then in horror as the hellish light showed the unconscious form of Brenda Phipps lying on the floor. He bent and grabbed her arm, intending to lift her over his shoulder as his training told him a fireman might do, but a questing flame licked round the door to find and singe his face and hair, so he settled for simply dragging her limp body away from the door, over to the relative safety of the window. He was fumbling with the catches of that when Reg Finch came bursting in through the flames.

Reg had had a problem too. A falling or flying something had struck him on the forehead, leaving him feeling distinctly groggy, yet his instincts gave him no thought of immediate escape from the fire, not until he'd assured himself that his colleagues were all right. He wrenched a curtain from its hangings, cast it over his head and shoulders, and charged through the flames on the landing.

Arthur Bryant saw the blood on Reg's forehead and the wild look in his eyes, and decided the situation needed a clear head – that was probably his head, so he took charge.

'Out through the window, Reg,' he shouted urgently. 'Come on. We haven't got all day. Jump. It's not far down. I need you down there to catch Brenda.' That last point was made with a scream of desperation in his voice. Arthur had realised he was faced with a problem not covered at all on his fire-fighting courses; that of what to do with an unconscious body one storey up when there's no ladder and no support outside. Necessity might dictate that one should just push it out of the window and let it drop, but this hardly seemed appropriate.

Arthur's words penetrated Reg's gradually clearing mind, and they made sense, so he quickly climbed on the window ledge, got his feet outside, turned on to his stomach, then lowered himself down feet first.

Arthur wrenched Brenda upright. She was surprisingly heavy, but another heave sufficed to get her stomach on the sill with her head and shoulders out of the window. He needed to hurry now, for opening that window had made a chimney for the flames, and it was drawing the fire into the room. Soon it would be a deadly inferno in which no one could live for long.

Brenda's clothes kept snagging on the window catch, but Arthur kept lifting and heaving until her body was more outside than in. Then he could grab her ankles and lower her down head first.

It was about this time that Brenda regained consciousness, and finding herself ignominiously being dangled upside down engendered in her sufficient alarm and fear to release an ear-shattering high-pitched scream.

'Reg!' Arthur shouted. 'Have you got her?'

'Yes. Let her go,' he heard in reply.

Arthur let go. Now he could make his own leaping escape. It looked dramatic, but that was the quickest way out, and he was none too soon, for a long hungry tongue of flame followed him through the window.

Ironically it was Brenda who untangled herself from the heap of sprawling bodies first.

'Reg, you saved my—' she started to say, but she was interrupted sharply.

'Don't thank me. You thank Arthur. If it wasn't for him you'd be an over-cooked sausage by now,' Reg declared. That might have been a marginal overstatement, but under the circumstances a little extra drama wouldn't be inappropriate. They were all safe, but things could easily have been a lot worse.

'Thanks, Arthur. I'll do the same for you one day,' Brenda announced in a rather choked voice as she reached down and helped pull her saviour to his feet. He just grinned at her, and silently set about unwinding the now unnecessary bandages from his head and then using them to wipe the smeared greasepaint from his face.

'Come on, you lot,' Reg said loudly so that his voice could be heard above the roar of the flames. 'Let's get out of here. The roof will fall in soon.'

So the rather battered trio made their way towards safety and the path to the Tudor wing, where they were joined by Walsh and his extended party.

'Are you three all right?' Walsh asked anxiously. 'You all look a bit the worse for wear to me. That's a nasty bump you've got on your head, Brenda.'

'I'm okay,' Brenda announced, bravely ignoring her headache, the bruises and a few stinging singes.

'I'm afraid our ambush was a failure, boss,' Reg said gloomily as he dabbed at the cut on his forehead with his handkerchief; yet even so, his eyes were bright with interest as he looked at the faces of the two additional members of Walsh's party.

'We can't win them all,' Walsh commented dourly.

'So it was a set-up. I thought it might be,' Robin Sainsbury said accusingly. 'And where is Andy Myres? He's all right, is he?'

'Myres is as snug as a bug, in hospital,' Walsh replied, watching Sainsbury's face closely. 'So you spotted our ambush, did you? Very perceptive of you. Well, this one didn't work, more's the pity. If it had, we might have laid our hands on Fitzpatten's killer. As it is, well, we could be faced with months of hard-grafting investigation, but we won't give up easily, I can assure you of that. Were you staying in the hotel tonight, Mr Sainsbury?'

Robin Sainsbury shook his head and he looked away. 'No, I went home, and then came back. I parked on the far side of the course, and walked in through the wood. Well, I crept in really, Red-Indian style,' he added with a reluctant half-smile.

'Well, we've still got some loose ends to tie up before we can go home, and you can help us, Mr Sainsbury, if you would. Reg, you take Arthur and Mr Sainsbury, and check the cars in the car-park at the front of the hotel. Just in case the killer hasn't made his escape yet. Brenda, Alison, and you too, Mr Finlay, we'll do

158

a four-person-wide sweep along the eighteenth fairway. Our quarry might have dropped something, you never know. If you don't look, you won't find, will you?' Walsh sounded, surprisingly, almost light-hearted.

'I'll go and get some torches,' Alison said as Reg and his party headed off to the car-park.

'Have you got one for me?' Grant Finlay asked when Alison returned.

'You won't need one,' Walsh said with a broad grin that was now clearly discernible in the light from the blazing building. 'That's all we'll need.' He pointed to the small black box that Alison was holding. It was bolted to a short aluminium rod, and had some wires coming from it.

'Eh! A metal detector? What's the good of that?' Finlay exclaimed with a frown.

'It's a Geiger counter, as a matter of fact. A gadget for measuring radioactivity.'

'Oh aye,' Finlay said phlegmatically, giving a shrug of his shoulders. 'Very useful, I suppose, if you work at a place like the Sellafield nuclear power station.'

Brenda gave a light laugh. 'That's true, but we spread a radioactive powder over the floor of the golf shop, Mr Finlay,' she explained. 'Our arsonist must have trodden on it, and will now have it on the soles of his shoes. Wherever that person has been treading faint traces will have been left behind. Only tiny ones, but the Geiger counter will pick them up. All we've got to do is to be like the Pied Piper's children, and happily follow where it leads us.'

'Strewth. So your damned ambush wasn't a failure after all. We're really going to get this bloody killer tonight, are we? That's a good thing. I don't like the idea of murderers wandering about just as they please. The sooner they're all locked up and behind bars, the better, but that radioactive stuff will wear off after a while, won't it? We'd better get a move on.' Finlay was agog with enthusiasm.

'No need to panic. In dry conditions we can follow it for about two miles. Less if it's wet, of course, but that doesn't matter.'

'We won't have that far to go,' Finlay announced sternly.

'Oh, so you think you know who it is, do you?' Walsh asked, looking at Finlay's face keenly.

159

'I had three or four people on my list until tonight, but now I'm down to one.'

'Reasoned, or just a guess?'

'Both, probably. It's when people don't do what you'd expect them to do, or what they do seems out of character. Something like that.'

'Maybe. Right, check weapons, then we'll be off,' Walsh said, taking his Smith and Wesson revolver from his shoulder holster, and spinning the chamber dramatically.

'Christ! I forgot that whoever it is has got a pistol. Here, you lot, be careful. Guns are dangerous and I don't want you shooting me. I may be getting old, but I like life too much.'

'You don't have to come, if you don't want to.'

'Of course I'm coming. Just you lot make sure you don't point them things at me.'

'We won't. Come on, let's go.'

Alison led the way. She had seen the path of the fleeing dark shadow earlier, so she was able to pick up the route quite easily. Even though she wore earphones, the clicks the little gadget made as she swung it from side to side were audible to the others.

The fact that they were all walking on the mown grass of a landscaped scene, in the moonlight of a lovely balmy May night, had no apparent romantic effects on this now stern and sombre party. Such things were irrelevant when one was out to hunt down a murderous killer.

It occasioned no surprise when Alison suddenly turned to her right, and led them towards the looming bulk of the hotel building, and the small door at the side that opened on to the back stairs.

They crept up those stairs and trod softly along the carpeted corridor. By a door with the number eleven on it, Alison suddenly stopped. She swung the Geiger counter round again to check, then switched it off and removed the earphones. A jerk of her head told them all that their quarry had gone into that room.

Brenda moved back down the corridor. 'Reg! On the first floor – the sixth room along, from your right, as you see it,' she breathed softly into her radio.

'I've got it. There's no light on, but the window is wide open.

160

Whoever is in there is most likely mighty nervous and jumpy. Be careful,' Reg warned.

Walsh, meanwhile, had tried to turn the door handle, but it was locked on the inside, and wouldn't move. That meant digging in his trouser pocket for the bulky duplicate set of hotel guest room keys he'd deemed it necessary to carry for just such an outcome to their ambush plans.

In spite of his being extremely careful while selecting the right one, there were a few metallic clicks that seemed unnervingly loud out there in the corridor. It was the same when the tumblers moved as he slowly inserted the key into the lock. Still, that could not be helped. He had been as quiet as anyone could be.

Now he was ready to thrust the door open. This was the most dangerous moment. Whoever was in there might be listening for any sound that meant the forces of law and order were coming to confront a murderer and an arsonist.

Brenda had her handgun drawn and ready, so too had Alison. His own would have to stay where it was, for he needed both hands to do what he had to do.

'No shooting unless a firearm is being aimed at any of us.' He breathed the warning softly to the others. Regulations required him to give those instructions, because he was in charge; and because he was in charge, he had to confront and challenge the armed person within, who, for all he knew, might even now have a pistol aimed at the door. He would not delegate that to anyone else, not if he still wanted to look at his own face in the mirror when he shaved each morning. There was no point in waiting longer, it was best to get it over.

He suddenly turned the door handle, pushed the door open wide and reached out to smack at the wall with his free hand where the light switches should be, then he jumped smartly to his right, out of the doorway.

'We are police officers,' he shouted as the room became a blaze of light. 'Stay still and don't—'

That was as far as he got. There was the muted crack of a firearm, and he heard something smack into the corridor wall behind him. The killer had obviously not disposed of the small-calibre handgun.

Brenda made a move as if to peer round the doorway, but Walsh's hand on her shoulder pulled her back. They were all

161

safe where they were in the corridor, and for the person within, there was no escape that way.

It was the three watchers concealed behind the cars in the car-park who now had their part to play, for things had already got too hectic for the person in the bedroom, and panic had taken over again. Reg Finch and Arthur Bryant, with Robin Sainsbury between them, saw a trousered figure appear momentarily at the open window, and from there it launched itself into space in a desperate leap that was even more elegant than Arthur's had been from the blazing building earlier. The landing wasn't quite as good though. The figure's feet crunched deep into the loose gravel and only outstretched hands prevented a full-length sprawl. What little light there was showed clearly that there was a gun held in the right hand.

'Drop that gun, and keep quite still,' Reg Finch yelled from behind a red Range Rover. 'You are surrounded, and we are armed. If you aim that gun at any of us we will have no choice but to shoot you. So drop it. Now!'

The figure straightened up from the ground and looked round wildly, as though still seeking a way of escape, but there was no obvious sign of one, and then its right hand started to come slowly up.

'No! No! Don't do it. Don't shoot,' Robin Sainsbury cried out fearfully as he pushed Arthur to one side and dashed forward, right into Reg Finch's line of fire.

The figure's right arm came up to point straight at the approaching man, and for a moment it held steady.

Sainsbury screamed out a name, and came on.

The figure gave a helpless cry of recognition. Tears started to flow from its eyes as a possible future of happiness suddenly became an unbearably black empty void – one that just couldn't be faced alone.

The gun was jerked back to be aimed at the figure's own head, and then it was fired.

Inside the hotel Sidney Walsh and Brenda Phipps rushed over to the bedroom window. There was plenty of light for them to see what was going on below.

The limp figure of Amanda Knightly was being cradled in the arms of a weeping and distraught Robin Sainsbury but, judging by the unnatural way her head appeared to be rolling from side to side, there was little he or anyone else could do to calm her distress this time.

Reg Finch bent down to rest a hand sympathetically on Sainsbury's shoulder.

Arthur Bryant looked up and saw the watchers at the window. His still grimy face was grim as he drew the fingers of one hand slowly and dramatically across his throat, and as if to make his meaning even more clear, he shook his head, and turned away.

The hotel's television lounge, not often a well-used facility, had become the unofficial meeting and refreshment centre for the forces of law and order, and even those of the emergency services. The few hotel night duty staff had coped remarkably well with the aftermath of fire engines and ambulances which had inevitably disturbed many of their guests from their slumbers. Some of those guests, unable to doze off again, had demanded coffee or tea, or even stronger liquor. Thus, when the police investigation team had dealt with those matters that had required their immediate attention, there was already a supply of such refreshments to hand, and the lounge, at the far end of the building, was the obvious place for the staff to serve them, albeit with frequent hushed exhortations for those there to keep their voices down, since there were some guests still asleep in the rooms above.

'Well, I haven't ever seen anything like it before, not in real life, I haven't,' Grant Finlay admitted, leaning back in a comfortable armchair and holding a steaming cup of coffee with both gnarled hands, its contents having been liberally garnished with a topping of fine brandy. 'I thought we were a tough bunch in the army, living a fine line between death and glory, but to you lot it all seems just another day's work. You stake out victims as bait for cunning murderers, leap from blazing buildings and end up with a shoot-out at the OK corral. Hang me if I won't apply for a job with you lot, it beats cutting grass any day.'

'Most of our work is boringly patient routine. I think you're exaggerating the excitement and the dangers a trifle,' Walsh suggested with a faint smile.

'You reckon?' Finlay responded. His face looked drawn and tired in the harsh lights of the lounge, but his eyes were alert and bright. 'For a trap like you set to work, you need lots of determination and training. They all play a big part, but so too does luck, and luck's a mighty chancy lady. She swings as easy one way as another. You three upstairs in Andy's flat, for instance . . .' He waved a hand towards Reg, Brenda and Arthur. 'You didn't know for sure what would happen. You could cope all right with a killer's knife or a cudgel perhaps, but I reckon that fire caught you unawares. It did me too, but what if it had been a bomb? What then? You might all be corpses right now, if luck had gone the other way.'

Reg's face reddened slightly, and he opened his mouth to say something, but Finlay hadn't finished talking. 'And then there was you,' he pointed a finger at Alison, 'haring off after someone you knew had a gun. If you'd got too close, what would have happened? She'd have turned round and shot you, wouldn't she? Robin here did you a favour when he stopped you in your tracks. You might be as dead as a dodo yourself right now.'

'There's risks and there's calculated risks. Alison was also armed, don't forget. Apprehending law-breakers is our job. Someone's got to do it. It's like what you were doing when you were in the army,' Walsh interrupted defensively.

'Don't get all worked up, mate. It's constructive criticism I'm giving you. When we'd done a job in Malaya we'd have a de-briefing session. Then we could say whatever we liked, or didn't like, as long as it was constructive. That way the next time we went out we might do things better, and maybe we'd live longer. You took a hell of a risk yourself tonight, when you kicked that bedroom door open, and you're the boss. Still, you got what you wanted, you've nailed your murderer, and that's what it's all about, isn't it? Myself, I think it's a good thing she shot herself like she did. It's what she did to young Gregory Fitzpatten, so now she knows what it feels like too. I know it's tough on you, Robin, but you're best out of it, really you are.'

Robin Sainsbury looked up from dejectedly staring at the backs of his hands. 'I knew there was something not quite right, when I first met her. I thought then that she might be a cold, hard man-hater, but as the golf round went on she seemed to relax and become quite friendly. I should have known better, even really unpleasant golfers can show their best side when things are going extra specially well for them, but at that bunker, when that fellow's hand came up out of the sand, she broke down just like a real normal woman. I couldn't help but feel sorry for her. She was so shocked she needed my help badly,' he said unhappily.

'You can understand, now, just how badly she was shocked,' Brenda Phipps said, glad that the conversation had turned away from the effectiveness of ambush plans, and people getting caught within blazing buildings. 'The night before, she'd just shot Fitzpatten dead, in his own sitting-room. A deed of revenge that had been playing on her mind for years, probably, and even more so when she found she'd been invited to the golf tournament, right next to where the hated man lived. That's when she started to turn her fantasy dreams into murder plans. When she walked out of the Tudor wing that night after killing him, she must have been on a real high. It had been so easy for her. Naturally, when a girl as attractive as she was rang Fitzpatten's front door bell, he would have invited her in, and turned on all his charm. We think she might have held out a framed photograph, and asked him if he recognised the face on it, and when he said yes – she shot him. The glass in the frame broke when he fell, and she might then also have dropped a small coin. Anyway, she just walked out of the front door, thinking that there was no way anyone could tie her in with the killing. There she was, one of dozens of guests in the hotel from all over the place, just there to play golf. Why should she be a suspect? As you say, the next morning she'd even started to relax enough to enjoy her game of golf. Then, in the Man Trap bunker, she came face to face with her victim again, where he never ought to be. I'm surprised she didn't flip her lid completely.'

'What's this revenge and photograph business got to do with it?' Grant Finlay asked.

'Her younger sister was one of Fitzpatten's conquests when he was up at the university,' Reg Finch explained. 'He ditched her eventually, just as he ditched all the others, but she couldn't cope – she just couldn't take it. She went home for the vacation and slashed her wrists. That's why Fitzpatten was killed. Revenge for her sister's suicide.'

'It sounds as though the whole family were half-way round the twist, but if she shot Fitzpatten in his own sitting-room, how the hell did he end up in the bunker?' Grant Finlay demanded.

'Well . . .' Walsh responded cautiously. That tale of Catholics and Jews, of secret passages, a peeping Tom, and the attempted sexual blackmail of the victim's widow, was not one for the ears of Finlay or Sainsbury. Bits of it might come out in the coroner's report or a subsequent enquiry, but that wouldn't be his problem. 'Someone else found Fitzpatten's body,' Walsh went on slowly, 'and that person jumped to the wrong conclusions about who his killer was, and decided to move it. That person must have known Fitzpatten was writing a book on Hitler, and may also have known enough about the history of the end of the Second World War to realise that Fitzpatten had been shot in the same way that Hitler had shot himself. So burying the body in a "bunker" may have seemed the cynically appropriate thing to do. Alternatively, having already dragged the body a long way, the Man Trap may simply have been the nearest and easiest place to put it. Either way it was confusing, because it set us looking for a homicidal religious maniac.'

'Eh!' Finlay exclaimed, his grey bushy eyebrows rising sharply.

'When Amanda Knightly had got over her initial shock,' Alison interrupted quickly, 'she just couldn't bring herself to leave the hotel, not until she'd found out what on earth had been going on. She needed a good excuse for doing that, because otherwise it might make her stand out from all the other hotel guests. The idea of needing to play sand iron shots out of that bunker to overcome her nightmares was all right, but if a bit of romance was added, it became a far better reason. Since you'd shown an obvious interest in her, you were the logical victim, I'm afraid, Mr Sainsbury.'

'And I fell for it, hook, line and sinker. She may have become a man-hater because of what Fitzpatten did to her sister, but she could still make herself extremely desirable . . . I think she did like me, in a way . . .' Sainsbury said ruefully.

'The act of killing can suddenly release a killer's repressed and pent-up feelings, and they can become quite uninhibited sexually. It's why some of them do it again. It's like being on a high for drug addicts,' Arthur Bryant volunteered, presumably having remembered some phrase from a book on criminal psychology. This piece of wisdom seemed to leave his listeners totally unmoved.

'It's understandable, Robin, you falling for her. You've been alone for a long while now, and you're at a vulnerable age. You

166

ain't the first man to make a fool of yourself over a pretty face, nor will you be the last. She weren't bad-looking, I'll give you that,' Finlay acknowledged. 'So, she was after finding out what you police people knew, then. That's what made me suspicious, the way she kept hanging about the eighteenth green. Obviously she couldn't relax until she found out who had moved Fitzpatten's body, because that person might have known it was her as done it, I suppose.'

'She changed too quickly from man-hater to warm joyous lover. People noticed it, and remarked on it, but you had her weighed up as the murderer pretty early on, had you, Mr Finlay?' Brenda asked politely.

'Not really. I was suspicious. There was a hardness about her, like someone with a real chip on her shoulder, when she weren't smiling and being all luvvy duvvy with Robin here. People who can change their face as quick as that can't be trusted. I've seen it before in folks, but to be honest, I was suspicious of more'n just her. I reckon that wife of Fitzpatten's had never come to terms with the fact that Gregory wasn't as besotted with her as all the other stupid men she flickered her eyelashes at, and he was still carrying on with other women too, just like she was with other men. That might have rankled her bad enough to kill him; and I'd got Houghton on my list because Gregory used to have it off with his wife regular like, and there was Stilito, and his daughter too.' He grinned. 'If you bet on all the runners in the field, you can hardly fail to get a winner.'

'What about you, Mr Sainsbury? I think you had your suspicions about her too. That's why you were out there watching tonight, and that's why you tackled Alison, when you saw her chasing Amanda Knightly. You wanted Amanda to get away, didn't you?' Reg Finch asked.

Robin Sainsbury nodded ruefully. 'I'm afraid so. I'm sorry. I got suspicious when I told her about Andy Myres having seen Fitzpatten's killer. I was watching her eyes, you see. It doesn't matter how poker-faced you try and be, your eyes can give you away. I saw fear and terror in hers then, and there could be only one reason for that. Even so, I didn't want to believe that she could have hated anyone enough to want to kill him.'

'Well, I can believe it. Love, hate, and madness – haven't I said that they've dogged the Fitzpatten family for generations? I reckon it won't be long before the folks around here see Gregory's ghost a-prowling and a-howling round the eighteenth green and the Man Trap bunker. Hand in hand with the old Middlemarch spook too, probably.' Finlay pushed himself to his feet. 'Well, dawn's coming up fast, and I've got work to do. That eighteenth green probably looks like a ploughed field, what with all the running around and fighting we've done on it tonight. I'd best go and try and get that lot sorted out before folks want to use it.'